Girl Wrapped in Branches

An Ella Porter Mystery Thriller

Georgia Wagner

Contents

Prologue

Rose took a hesitant step up the moldered dock, her foot creaking against the wooden boards. Her heart pounded, and her ears perked, attentive for even the slightest sound of warning.

She wasn't supposed to be here, but the temptation had been too strong.

The young woman paused, listening, but all she heard was the quiet lapping of crystal-clear water against the wooden support posts.

The scent of the liquid hovered on the air, intermingling with the fresh fragrance of the surrounding, ancient forest. Rose Lewis ran a hand through her dark hair, smoothing bangs behind her ears.

A sound behind her—a sudden splash.

She whirled about, heart leaping in her throat. Ripples extended from the water nearest the shore, spreading out against the stones in pulses. She stared, frowning hesitantly, discerning the source of the disturbance in the sacred lake.

Her eyes moved up the shore, pausing. The long roots of enormous, ancient trees protruded through the mud and muck, spreading down the shore towards the lake, dipping the boughs into the liquid. Some of the roots were wider than she was. She'd never seen such large trees before.

But that was part of the appeal of this place, wasn't it?

She shivered, feeling the wind pick up.

The ripples from the splash had subsided now, and she spotted a culprit. A branch in the water. She bit her lip, staring at the thing and shaking her head.

"It's nothing. No one's here," she murmured to herself, trying to calm her fraying nerves.

She forced a quick smile, if only to ease herself and turned back to the water, reaching into her pocket and pulling out the small, wax candle she'd brought with her. With another urgent look over her shoulder, back towards the entrance to the dock, her eyes trailed over the chain she'd slipped under, moving past the wooden sign with bright, white painted letters that simply read: *Forbidden*.

In the heart of inland Alaska, reaching towards the end of October, very few places were nearly so temperate or warm.

This was why they called the place an oasis. A hundred miles north of Nome, the small, idyllic lakeside community of Parcel wasn't known to most. This was intentional.

The residents here, a combination of settlers and natives who lived in harmony, didn't *want* outsiders encroaching on their small slice of paradise. The mountains surrounding the village, creating a valley out of the peaks, protected the town from the harsher inclinations of Alaskan weather. The hot springs bubbling up at the foot of Mount Sherman also helped warm Parcel.

A temperate, warm, vibrant lake town in the heart of Alaska also served as an attraction for wildlife who could drink year-round from the melted lake.

It attracted other sorts too...

Not just bucks and badgers, wolves and bears...

But people like Rose Lewis. Outsiders... She was expressly forbidden from touching the lake—no less placing a wish, but she was out of options. Her boyfriend had brought her to this place, after all. He'd shown her Parcel. Had shown her the lake, forbidden though it was by the ruling elders of the small town.

With trembling fingers, she pulled her lighter from her pocket, flicking the flame a few times until it ignited. She raised the thing and placed it to the small candle, willing the wick to catch. She'd brought the candle with her, made of beeswax, just like the legend required.

She hesitated, biting her lip, trying to remember the incantation... She'd even written the words down on her phone in case she forgot, but they sprung to her memory like bubbles released from silt.

She hesitated, exhaled briefly, then said, "*From the earth. From the moon. From the heart. From the womb.*" She nodded and ignited the candle. The wind blew it out.

She frowned, tried again. The wind blew it out again.

She scowled now. A bad omen.

Another creaking sound behind her. She shot a quick look back. A shape behind the trees?

"Who's there?" she called out.

No answer.

She shook her head—no, just a trick of the light. She forced a quick chuckle, a smile, then shielded the candle with her body against the wind, ignited the wick a final time, waiting for it to catch. Once the blaze started, she stared down at the small pinprick of flickering light, wishes brought to mind once more.

She lowered the candle onto the lake, slowly, gingerly.

This was the most difficult part.

If the candle floated, the wish would come true.

If it sunk, though?

Calamity.

The omens were clear—her boyfriend had told her everything about Parcel. The smiling, pleasant people. Very communal, like the Amish in some ways—averse to outsiders. But friendly, kindly. They didn't advertise their town, and in fact, kept their name off most maps.

But that didn't mean they weren't hospitable sorts...

Mostly.

But her boyfriend had told her *other* things about his family and some of the people in Parcel.

"Accept me..." whispered Rose, setting the candle with trembling fingers on the water. The small, buoyant, aluminum sheath would serve to float the thing. She balanced it and paused, watching the flickering flame, and then, with a wince, released.

It floated, carried tardily on the lazy current, washed further out towards the middle of the lake. She wondered how many other candles had snuffed out in the middle, before being claimed by the water.

How many hundreds if not thousands of wishes had been offered in the heart of Parcel?

There were other methods, according to her boyfriend, and the multi-generation traditions. But some had made her squeamish, and the one involving the hot springs would have been too expensive.

She watched, elated as her candle was carried away, towards the center of the lake...

And then it began to tip, to tilt. The flame singeing the yellowish wax black all of a sudden. She stared, stunned. The candle continued to tilt. "N-no!" she protested, but her words didn't matter.

She remained crouched at the end of the forbidden dock, kneeling against old, moldered wood, inhaling the scent of the lake while her heart sunk like a stone.

And the candle was soon to follow.

It toppled all of a sudden, with a faint *hiss,* then silence.

And then the small, aluminum base, and the beeswax candle was swallowed by the water.

The forbidden lake had rejected her plea. Rose felt tears forming in her eyes... She'd wanted children for years, but after the doctor's fertility report... this had seemed like the only way.

She shivered, hesitantly reaching back towards her pocket, pressing at the empty pouch where the candle had initially been. She hadn't brought a second—this, her boyfriend had said, was strictly forbidden.

But she was trespassing already, wasn't she?

An outsider performing a ceremony that belonged to the members of Parcel. She wasn't a local—she didn't have roots. She was just desperate.

And now her candle had sunk.

"What do you think you're doing?" a voice called out.

She whirled around with a squeak, startled, staring up at the treeline. She didn't see anyone. She shifted uncomfortably, glancing one way, then the other.

"I—I'm sorry. I'm lost!"

"You're robbing from us?" said the same voice, shaking with anger.

"No! No, I swear I'm not!"

"Don't lie to me, Rose," the voice murmured.

She still couldn't place the source of the voice nor did she recognize it, but the murmur of her name sent chills up her spine. They knew her...

"I—I'm sorry," she said desperately, wiping a tear from her eye. "I didn't mean to!"

She heard swishing, swaying. A few leaves tumbled. She still couldn't see the source of...

She looked slowly up and froze.

The long, thick branches extended over the water. The hundred-year-old trees carried some boughs as large as most conifers. But now, her eyes settled on a figure staring down at her. Two bright eyes and a dark shadow, nearly twenty feet in the air, straddling the branch...

And lowering something?

She blinked, staring, wrinkling her nose in confusion, trying to raise an apologetic hand. Trespassing—her boyfriend had warned her against trespassing...

What was it he'd said exactly?

If they find you... run.

She trembled, swallowed... The person on the tree branch far above dropped something. It fell, slapping against her face and she let out a faint yelp. She stumbled away from it, but stared at where a thick knot and loop of rope dangled.

As she distanced herself, staring at the rope, she wrinkled her nose in confusion as the rope suddenly moved, swinging towards her and bumping against her nose, then grazed her cheek, the fibers rough against her smooth skin.

She tried to push it away, her hand tangling in the coarse hemp, murmuring, "I'm sorry! I'll—I'll just be going. I shouldn't have come... I'm sorry!"

She took a step forward, trying to duck under the thing now and dash towards the shore but then the person above yanked the rope *hard*.

A noose. She hadn't realized in the dark what knotted the far end. But the noose wrapped around her arm, going taut, yanking hard around an outstretched limb, and she yelled, emitting a shout of horror. The rope bit into her wrist, and she screamed.

She tried to run now... but far, far too late.

The spider's web had caught the fly.

And now she was trapped. As she ran, her arm jerked behind her, still trapped. It pulled hard—suggesting the person above had wrapped the rope around the branch.

They'd moved so quietly up the branch—hung there so naturally, as if it suited them the way a sidewalk suited rubber soles.

Rose screamed as the rope began to pull. Her arm still taut, her wrist caught, she yanked and tugged like a fish on a hook. And then she slipped, the rope pulled harder. She hit the worn dock, struggling to rise. The rope tightened again.

She flopped about, desperate, yelling. And then the rope began to pull, faster, harder, yanking her *up, up, up.*

"SORRY!" she screamed. "I'M SORRY!"

But her words were lost to the wind. The mountains shielded Parcel from the elements but also prying eyes. Her boyfriend had warned her about the strange things that happened in this place.

The disappearances.

And she should have listened. The tears now dried on her cheek as she was yanked higher, higher into the air. The person on the branch above her matching the place where they were situated in sheer *strength.* She flailed about, kicking, scratching at her wrist, but the rope was just too tight.

And now, above her, those leering eyes and a flash of silver.

The eyes fixated on her, the silver—a blade—clutched in a taut hand. She continued to scream as she was pulled off the dock, dangling over the forbidden, sacred lake, and carried up into the spider's web.

Chapter 1

Ella's gun pointed directly at the Graveyard Killer's skull. She stood in her small, cheap, stinking motel room, glaring at the man. It took her a second to realize she wasn't breathing. She exhaled shakily. The puff of air lifted stray blonde bangs which had fallen over her eyes; these, pure blue and resembling frozen rain.

The man on the bed studied her, wearing his neat, pressed suit with silver cuff-links. His thinning hair was combed to the side, and as he watched her, there was something strange about his eyes. An emptiness and darkness like deep hollows in the earth with no end in sight.

Alone in the motel room, her back to the door, Ella eased back until her spine bumped against the cold handle.

"I told you not to come," she said, her voice shaking. Just as quickly, she inhaled, her expression turning into a mask. She couldn't remember the last time she'd lost her temper, and even now, she wasn't about to let *this* man, this serial killer, unnerve her.

He sat unarmed, save the remote in his hand, which he aimed at the television. Occasionally, he'd wince or grimace, or grin as the cricket match swung one way then the other. He muttered, "Come on, now—faster! Faster!" He frowned, shaking his head in frustration, watching the television completely now.

He didn't even seem to notice the gun pointed at his head. The same way he didn't seem to notice his foot resting on the head of a dead man, lying face down on her bed. The discarded pillow against the ground, resting on a stained carpet, suggested the murder weapon.

Ella tried to piece it all together. The corpse on the bed was unfamiliar to her, but evidently, the Graveyard Killer had snuck up on him in the small motel room, murdering him on her bed. Which only left the question... Why was this second strange man *in her bedroom* to begin with?

"Did you bring him here?" she said, her gun jolting down briefly.

The Graveyard Killer gave a sudden cheer, smiling like a school boy. "Yes! That's the ticket! Ha!"

"Hey!" she said, her voice rising.

He looked over now suddenly, wincing sheepishly. "Apologies—where are my manners." He cleared his throat delicately, raised the remote and clicked off the television. Then, he folded his hands on his lap, adjusting a bit, still using the corpse as a footstool.

"Eleanor," he said, watching her with a look of extreme pleasure. "You are as lovely as I remember."

"Why are you here?"

He shook his head. "I told you. We need to chat."

"About what? There's nothing to chat about. Did you kill him?"

"Yes."

"Alright, get up. I'm taking you in."

He didn't rise. "Now, Eleanor, please. This man was hiding in your motel room, armed with a gun—see, I left the weapon over there." He nodded across the room.

She risked a quick glance, spotting where a handgun was set neatly on a small coffee table under the television. The clip removed. Each bullet sitting upright, organized in a perfect sequence, one next to the other. Not a single one of the little, metal soldiers out of line.

It was telling that the Graveyard Killer hadn't kept the gun on him. Though, perhaps, he had one of his own. From her memories, hunting him across the lower forty-eight, however, he preferred using his hands.

"Why was he here?" she asked quietly.

"I tried to ask him, but he was already a bit... preoccupied." The well-dressed man flashed a crocodile grin. Those same, deep, hollow eyes watched her, unblinking. "I believe he meant to harm you, Eleanor. You look in a rough way, my dear."

She frowned at him. She didn't like the familiar way he was speaking to her. But he wasn't wrong. Yesterday had been a difficult one. She'd nearly drowned, nearly frozen, then nearly been stabbed. She'd managed to rescue her young cousin, Madison Porter, though. At least there was that.

She said, "I'm fine."

"Now that's disappointing. I thought we were going to be honest with one another." He gave a little wiggle of his feet, his expensive loafers shifting and catching sheen from the light creeping through the blinds. "Any idea who my new friend is?" he asked, conversationally.

"I'm not the one who killed him," she shot back. "Now get up. I mean it—I'm taking you in."

He frowned, puzzled. "Whatever for?"

She stared. "You just killed someone."

"He was going to kill *you*," the man said slowly. He took another grape from the bowl next to him, popping the fruit into his mouth and chewing slowly. He shook his head. "Really, I saved your life."

Ella thought back to the man who'd taken a shot at her the previous day on the mountain. Twice, in fact—two bullets. Both missed because of her quick thinking. She hadn't known who the assassin had been at the time. Now... she supposed she knew.

She stared at the dead man. "Still have his phone?"

"Yes. Would you like it? A peace offering."

"I told you not to come here." But Ella still stepped forward, reaching out to accept the phone offered to her. A sleek, silver device which the intruder held out benevolently. She hesitated, watching him closely to make sure he wouldn't lunge, and then stepped in quick, gun held back in case he went for it, snatched the phone and retreated.

He didn't so much as flinch but kept watching her.

It was his cold confidence that most unhinged her. Sitting in the motel room of an FBI agent, feet on a corpse he'd killed, casually admitting he'd done so.

"You seem upset," he said slowly. "This?" he pointed towards his feet. "If it helps, think of it as self-defense. He *did* have a gun. And I was unarmed. Well... I mean, unless you count the pillow."

Ella glanced again at the discarded pillow. She swallowed, her skin prickling as she retreated once more to the door, her back against the doorknob again, the silver phone clutched in her off hand, her gun still pointed towards the bed. "I told you to get up."

"But you don't mean it, Eleanor."

She shook her head. "I do. Now. *Up!*" Her voice hardened.

So did his eyes. He looked no longer like a schoolboy but almost like a disapproving father. He watched her, rigid. "Don't take that tone with me, Eleanor. We've been through too much. Or have you so quickly forgotten? This isn't the first time I've saved your life. You *owe* me."

She winced. "I don't. We're even. I let you go."

"That? You did that for *you,* not for me. We both know it." Now, he flung his legs over the bed, moving slowly, on the side furthest from her, as if not wanting to startle her. He stood upright as she tensed but didn't even glance at her. Briefly, he adjusted his suit sleeves, smoothing the front and dusting himself off a bit.

She watched as, back still to her, he procured a small lint roller from inside his jacket and tended to his sleeves. He ran the lint roller down his pant legs then straightened, peeled off the single wedge of sticky paper covered in lint a few of Ella's blonde hairs which must have been left on the bed, and then tossed the paper into the waste bin by the desk.

Then, stowing the lint roller, he turned to look at her.

He was of average height, about the same age as her father, with pleasant, symmetrical but unremarkable features. He frowned now at the gun as if he found the item offensive; he stepped around the jutting legs of the dead man on the bed and, still frowning, opened his mouth to say something.

But before he did, his phone began to ring. He winced, sighed, checked the device and winced again. "Pardon me," he said quickly, holding up a finger. He then turned away briefly, shifting and answering the phone, concealing his lips with his shoulder.

In a soft, muffled voice, he said, "Darling, daddy's working. Hmm? Oh yes, my sweet, as much as you'd like. No—did you ask your mother?" A hesitant pause, as if listening to some long response. "Alright then—soon, princess. A few days, maybe less. I promise." He chuckled, shaking his head. "You are my moon and stars... Right now? I'm afraid I'm in a meeting. What if I sing it to you later tonight, before you go to sleep? No, dear, it's mummy's turn to read to you. Alright. Yes, I love you too!" He laughed in delight. "Until we meet again," he said in a mock, dramatic voice. "Good night, my sweet." He cleared his throat, lowered his phone, then turned, his facial features readjusting.

"Sorry," he said with a little cough, shrugging sheepishly.

"I let you go once," Ella replied, deciding to ignore the call completely. Some rocks were best left settled. "I'm not about to do it again."

"It is a risk I'm willing to take," he replied softly. "Twenty so far."

"Twenty?"

"Young women, mostly. It's been hard for me to find out much more than that. They don't take kindly to outsiders." He watched her now, his voice a low rasp. Something else had entered his gaze, something that sent shivers up Ella's spine—something colder, even, than the blizzard she'd weathered yesterday.

Ella exhaled. "No—no, don't try it again. I fell for it once, not this time."

"Fell for it? I'm not lying. You know I'm not."

"You've killed seventeen people! Eighteen!" she exclaimed, gesturing with the assassin's phone towards his corpse.

"I've saved many more," he said. "You included. You know that. We've been over this before, Eleanor. And this new killer? He's murdered twenty young women. At least. It could be *much* more."

"Tell me who, then. I'll arrest them tonight."

He shook his head, troubled now. "I don't know who. They're hiding in this small town—Parcel, they call it. It's inland from here, about a hundred miles."

Ella huffed in frustration. "And how do you *know* that?" she snapped.

He winked at her. "Now that would be telling, wouldn't it?"

"No—not this time. I let you get away with coy last time. Tell me, or I'm marching you into the police station. I mean it!"

He leaned back now, his head tilting up, his eyes on her. Up to this point, he'd spoken politely, mannered and calm. But now a storm entered his voice. His words became colder, harder, brittle things, as if they might drop and shatter into sharp splinters. "You're wasting my time and yours! Grow up and help the adults or get the hell out of my way!" His eyes blazed and began moving towards her.

She kept her gun centered on his chest. "Don't! I'll shoot. STOP!"

He ignored her entirely, again, indifferent to the gun. Their shoulders touching, his arm grazing hers as he reached for the door handle.

She wanted to shove him—wanted to fire... but in another way, she really didn't. She knew what sort of man this was. Had known. And had made the same decision. She'd uncuffed him, let him go. She'd lost everything over it.

But now, with him trying to slip past her, refusing to lay a finger on her, Ella's jaw clenched in annoyance.

She knew his personal code well enough. She'd tracked him for years, hadn't she? It had been an obsession for some time. He didn't throw the first punch—he didn't react violently. Not until he was given reason.

Then he would move fast. Shockingly fast.

The trigger under Ella's finger strained, not quite pulled, not completely released.

Chapter 2

A shot to the gut; Ella's knee snapping forward towards his groin while her free hand swung for his throat. One lightning-quick, concerted attack. The only chance to take the Graveyard Killer down without a fight. Anything less and he would fight back, and if he fought back, she would have to kill him.

And so she didn't strike him, didn't fire her gun, because she didn't want to kill him.

The man might have walked like a gentleman in a suit, but he was something far more uncivilized underneath it all. He would fight tooth and nail like a bobcat caught by its tail if he thought he was cornered. And in the end, only one of them would emerge alive.

And she didn't want him dead.

So she stepped back.

He began to open the door, the light from the sun warming the room, both in illumination as well as temperature. A faint, fresh breeze spread through the cheap motel room, and Ella inhaled slowly, feeling a shred of relief wash over her simply due to the elements.

"Wait!" she said suddenly. "Wait, alright—I'm listening."

He paused, turning to look at her, adjusting his cuff-links. He nodded once.

The door clicked shut behind him.

And now he was standing against it with Ella having shuffled back, further in the room, now underneath the television. She pointed at the man on the bed. "Was it really self-defense?"

He said, "Does it matter?"

"To me, yes!" she yelled. "I'm not a criminal."

"You've done criminal things. You let me go," he pointed out. "And you will again."

"You're very confident I'm not going to arrest you."

"You haven't. You could have shot me. You could have had police waiting for me at every port and airfield when I arrived. It isn't like one can reach Nome by anything other than plane or boat."

Ella was breathing heavily now, and she didn't like to hear her own exhalations in her ears. The man wasn't very large but he was taller than her. She'd always been small, slight. She'd made up for it, not only with one of the best closure rates in the FBI, but with a will of steel.

But a part of her took risks—*enjoyed* the adrenaline rush of dangerous choices. Holding her breath beneath an icy sea in order to see how long she might last until passing out was one thing. But now, facing a man in the room who had just killed someone... this was a step over the line.

But she believed him when he said he'd killed an assassin who'd come for her.

He'd saved her life once before—this was also true.

But more than that... It was what he *did* that had allowed her to uncuff him. The reason he stalked the world, searching for *them*.

"Give me your name," she said suddenly. "At least give me that. Then we can talk."

He smiled now, hesitating. "You really didn't try to find out? After everything?"

"I found you but not your name."

"Interesting. I have so many questions about that evening."

"Yeah, well, answer mine first. I can't just go around calling you the Graveyard Killer."

He wrinkled his nose, his British accent growing thicker for a brief second. "How very Am... so very droll," he said distastefully. She'd wondered if he'd been about to say *American* instead, but then in order to remain polite, he'd switched halfway. She wasn't sure she even knew what *droll* meant.

This was something the two of them shared. A desire not to offend in polite conversation.

But other things they didn't share.

"Graves," he said simply. "You can call me Mr. Graves. Mortimer Graves." He chuckled at his own humor.

Ella swallowed. "Alright. Mortimer, a bit on the nose, don't you think?"

"It was my grandfather's name."

"I don't believe you."

"You probably ought not."

Ella still couldn't quite understand the man across from her. "Are you here to... to kill someone else?" she said slowly. "I can't help you, Mr... umm... Mr. Graves."

"No," he said, suddenly. "I'm here to hunt a monster. Just as I've always done."

"Is that what you call it?"

He frowned. "And what do you call it?"

She hesitated. "You're a serial killer. You've murdered seventeen men."

"That's not how you saw it a few months ago. You understood what I was doing."

"I didn't understand. I was tired. And... you *had* saved my life. I was feeling a bit grateful."

"That's not why you let me go," he replied. "We both know why you did it."

Ella stared at him, shaking. Her gun was still clutched in her hand, extended, but it no longer felt true... as if the raised weapon itself was a bluff. And they both knew it. So she lowered her arm, staring. She shifted uncomfortably in her sweater and slacks. Her clothing wasn't nearly as nice as his—most everything she owned was old, outdated. The phone in her hand, from the assassin on the bed, was at least six generations newer than the one in her pocket.

The two of them, facing each other, couldn't have been more dissimilar. Ella only ever wore simple, silver earrings. She didn't like jewelry. Didn't like expensive things. The cuff links on Mortimer's wrists were more expensive than her car back in the states... Of course, she hadn't been able to drive her old vehicle to Nome.

And yet as different as the two of them were, one on either side of a line known to most as "law enforcement," there was one thing they both shared.

An unsatiated desire to hunt murderers.

Mortimer Graves was a monster hunter, in his own mind. He caught killers—serial killers, murderers, rapists... the ones who got away with their crimes. Especially the repeat offenders.

He then took them... often *did things* to them. And left them dead on the gravestones of their victims.

This was how she'd found him. She'd discovered *who* he'd been hunting. She'd been one step ahead of the rest of the agents assigned to the case. One step ahead, even, than her partner at the time.

"Do you know how I found you?" she said quietly.

His eyebrows flicked up. "No," he said softly. "Pray tell." He ran a finger through his neatly combed, thinning, silver hairline, making sure not a strand was out of place.

"It wasn't by your name—we've established that. Not by DNA, none of it."

"So how?"

"Because I found your prey first."

He nodded. "You spotted the pattern."

"I knew you were tracking him."

"He'd killed, what, six girls by then?"

"Seven," Ella said reflexively. She pictured the smiling, young faces. Their sweet expressions. She knew their names. Knew the names of their schools. Knew the dates they'd been taken. What had been done to them. And where they'd ended up.

And as those memories flashed through her mind, her stomach curdled, and she wanted to sob. Instead, she said, shakily, "I went after the next victim."

"My next? So you found the pervert first."

She shook her head. "No. I found the girl he was targeting. I got there first. That's how I found him. The... the pervert."

"I see. I'm impressed. To find me, you found another killer." He threw back his head and laughed but then quickly pressed fingers to his lips. "I beg your pardon. But you have to see the humor in it, Eleanor Porter. Most were looking for me. But you didn't just look for the man I was hunting. You looked for the child *he* was hunting. Bait swallows bait swallows bait. Clever... Very clever. It must have taken you many sleepless nights to piece it all together."

"A week."

"Impressive."

"No... It took me months. But I didn't sleep for a week within those months. I needed the extra hours. I needed to figure out *where* you were going next. There were two options. But you always did have a soft spot for those targeting girls."

His eyes flashed. "Soft spot? No..." he said slowly. "I simply enjoy the smell of the freshly turned earth when I bury their godforsaken corpses." He didn't smile, didn't blink. "No soft spot."

"You know what I mean."

25

"I do. I also know you got a step ahead of yourself. What was the pervert's name again? Actually, no—I don't care. I don't want to know. He nearly strangled you, Ella. You're fortunate I arrived in time."

She nodded. Remembering the rain. The graveyard. Remembering how she'd followed that red car in the mist. Remembered watching it outside little Violet's suburban home. But she'd been spotted. The *pervert* as Mortimer called him had been spooked. Had fled. She'd thought she had him... But he'd ambushed her. A close thing... she'd nearly died.

But then the Graveyard Killer had arrived. She'd caught two killers the same night... Except it had nearly ended far worse.

"Why did you do it?" she said suddenly. "Why save me? You could have left. You could have waited for him to kill me then taken him out. You could have done all of it."

"I told you already."

"No, you said because you liked my hair. That wasn't an answer. Tell me for real and then we can talk about Parcel."

He shrugged once. "Because, Eleanor, it is *what I do.* I saved you for the same reason I hunted the pervert. The same reason I buried all of them. I don't remember their names. Not like you seem to. No one will remember their names. No one except the parents, the loved ones, the wives, the husbands, the brothers, the sisters of the victims they leave behind. The generations of children, offspring, others, children's children that perished along with the victims." He spoke in a tight-lipped

26

rhythm, a slow, resonant cadence. "I hunt them because they need to be hunted. The same as a mountain lion gone man-eater. The same as a badger with rabies. The same as a venomous spider in the bedroom." He glanced towards the assassin then back at her. "I hunt monsters. And that's why you let me go. Because you knew I was doing the right thing."

Ella wanted to retort. To object. She didn't know this at all.

But she'd done the math. While figuring out *who* the Graveyard killer was targeting, she'd discovered *how many* people had lived who might have died. One murderer had targeted a woman every month for a year. The police were nowhere near catching him.

Until Mortimer found him first. Mortimer had done things—horrible things—to the man's body, while he was still alive. Then left him on the tombstone of his last victim.

Sasha Byle. Ella didn't forget names.

She'd done the math. The average killer with that particular predilection would go on for years until caught. Twenty-four more victims? Thirty-six?

Not to mention the others. Rapists damaged the flesh but also the soul. Serial killers damaged their victims, but also, with a ripple effect, smashed families, entire communities. Robbed children of mothers, fathers. Robbed children *from* parents. Devastating what they touched.

27

It was a cold, heartless arithmetic, she'd felt. But she'd decided that Mortimer Graves had saved nearly a hundred lives. He'd taken seventeen, every one of them a monster.

But even monsters... could love, could heal...

And so she faced another impossible choice. She couldn't let him walk a second time. Could she? *How* could she?

She grimaced, wanting nothing more than to turn and run. To hide. She didn't want to face this horrible choice a second time. Once had been more than enough.

"You should leave," she said, shakily. "Leave, please. Don't come back. Don't ever let me see you again."

He held up a finger. "What if," he said softly, "we do it your way?"

"What?"

"I have another. One that you've missed. That *all* of them have missed. They've killed at least twenty."

"So you've said."

"But we can do it *your* way," he replied. "You help me find him. Help me enter this town, using that badge of yours. And I won't touch a hair on his head. You have my word."

She stared at Mortimer. "You... you want to help me... *arrest* him?"

He nodded once, crossing a finger over his heart. "I swear it on my eldest daughter," he said simply. And there was a note to his voice that she hadn't heard yet. A tremor of... of some emotion she couldn't place.

Ella swallowed. "So you'll tell me what you know, how you know it?"

"I won't tell you how. But I will tell you what. And then we do it your way. All I've ever wanted is to rid this world of this blight. Behind a cage or in the ground... I can live with either. And if the trial fails to indict." He smiled at her, flashing perfectly white teeth. "Then we try it my way."

"No!" Ella snapped, her heart leaping. "Never your way. *Never.*"

He shrugged.

"Promise me," she said, trembling. "Promise me you won't kill anyone else. You'll let me arrest them. Promise!"

He looked her dead in the eyes, stepped towards her, and whispered, "I swear on everything and everyone I love and cherish, when we find who is doing this, I will not touch a single hair on their head. We will do it your way."

He stepped back, giving a quick nod of his head, almost like a formal bow.

Ella wanted to refuse. Wanted to yell at him. Still wanted to drag him away in cuffs... But another part of her knew the truth.

If he went down, so did she. If he went to prison, so would she. She'd let him go. She'd been an accomplice to murder. And now, she shot another look towards the dead man on her bed—the man who'd come to kill her.

Who *would* have killed her if she'd wandered into the motel, exhausted, tired and alone.

Twice now, Mortimer had saved her life.

Twice...

And now the promise? The pinky swear to do it by the book?

He was making it so very, very easy for her to deceive herself. But deception in a favored direction often was an easy thing.

Ella felt shivers in her chest, her stomach tight.

But she couldn't forget those six names. And the seventh they'd saved. Couldn't forget all those others who he'd reached before she had. How many more girls, women, men would have lost their lives... had their souls cut and gouged and hurt...

It was so very easy to convince herself.

So why did it feel like a lead weight in her gut?

"Fine. My way," she said sharply. "And you stay back."

"I will never harm you, Eleanor."

Her eyes flashed, and in a grim tone, she replied. "But I might harm you. So stay back. Tell me exactly what you know, and what it is you want from me."

Chapter 3

Ella slammed the door to the field office's only work vehicle. The sun warmed her skin, and she inhaled the fresh air. Any other time, it might have been a pleasant stroll from the car, down the sidewalk, to the door of the small, flat-roofed home.

But now, a frown curdled her expression, and her gloved fingers twisted nervously at the hem of her secondhand jacket. She affixed her ever-present, pleasant smile though, as she approached the trailer's door. She reached out, hesitant, eyeing the streaked frame.

Ella had always considered herself something of an *amateur* germaphobe, as she would never want to encroach on the territory of the true pros who carried bottles of sanitizer wherever they went and would only open doors with elbows.

But as she examined this particular trailer's door, she felt a slow inkling to go pro.

She winced, exhaled, and then knocked with her gloved hand. She then took a step back, snow crunching underfoot—the remnants of the blizzard and a yet-to-be shoveled sidewalk.

Granted, outside *this* particular home, she assumed shoveling was a very rare occurrence.

The overflowing recycling bin around the side of the house was testament to the frequency of chores. The many brown bottles spilling over the lip of the blue bin, many having been smashed on the ground, served as testament to the *source* of the housekeeping procrastination.

Fragments of auburn glass caught the sunlight, winking at her from their downy bed of white fluff.

She looked away, tapping her foot and checking her phone again. Three calls, and he still wasn't answering.

"Come on," she muttered, tapping her foot nervously. She glanced back over her shoulder, as if expecting a police car to roll up behind her any moment.

A lifetime spent on one side of the law meant that venturing beyond those borders allowed a pit to settle in her gut.

She shot another look over her shoulder. A couple were strolling down the street, heading to the wharf, one of them pointing out the large crabbing vessel currently being used to cut through a crust of ice.

"What?" a voice snapped.

She turned sharply, smile still affixed.

The man in the door was bald, boasting a large belly and stained sweatpants. His double-chin wobbled as he burped and a few suspicious lumps along the side of his neck shifted as he scratched at them with chewed-on fingernails.

"Hello, Mr. Gunn," she said politely. "My name is—"

"Mrs. Porter, I know," snapped the man in the door, his shoulders slouched. "What do you want?" he spoke curtly, direct, clearly disinterested in her and anything she had to say.

She hesitated again. "I'm... I'm not Priscilla, I'm—"

"Look, I don't give a shit. Do I look like a duster? Huh? Think I'd live here if I was a miner? No—so you stay to your pretty side of the—" He paused and hiccupped, but then continued. "Of the town, and leave me to mine." He added a nod that could easily have been interpreted as *so there!*

She blinked at him, hesitant. "I... see..." She frowned.

Mr. Gunn, Brenner's father, had never gained a reputation as a nice man. Some said his wife had contracted cancer only to escape his fists. And now, judging by the state of him, and the smell of him, he'd already started, bright and early, partaking in brewer's poison.

She sighed, trying not to glance past him at the empty pizza boxes and discarded glass bottles across the floor. "Sir, I don't mean to bother you—"

"Good." He shut the door.

Her mouth was still open, preparing to speak, but the loud rattle of the metal door slamming left her temporarily speechless. She hesitated, tongue inside her cheek. She called out, "I'm looking for your son! His neighbor said he was here!"

The door remained closed.

She sighed, taking a few steps around the trailer to glance along the alley created by it and the opposite domicile. Then she heard rustling and stepped back as a man emerged, carrying two large trashbags with blue stickers attached to them. He hefted both as he marched towards the curb.

Brenner Gunn's lips were moving rapidly as he stared at the ground, earbuds settled in his ears, trailing down to his phone in his pocket. Even from where she stood, she heard the sound of loud rap music. His lips didn't speak but moved in rhythm with the cadence of the lyrics.

She watched him curiously as he dropped the two bags, turned, still mouthing the lyrics, and spotted her.

His lips went still and he blinked.

She winced and gave a polite wave.

The handsome six-foot man pulled the earbuds from his ears and one of his hands snuck into his pocket, hastily muting the music. The germaphobe in Ella winced at the hands which had touched garbage bags now moving to a device often pressed to one's face. But she held her tongue.

"Uh, hey," Brenner said, nodding awkwardly.

She watched him briefly. The two of them had dated nearly twelve years ago, and while most high school romances were passing fancies, she'd never quite been able to forget Brenner Gunn. The fact that the two of them had survived a blizzard together, Ella at points in her undergarments, had also created something of a strange bond between them.

Brenner had aged like wine—prettier now than he'd been then. But sadder too. Those blue eyes, that chiseled jaw, were somehow only aided by the single burn mark traced under the side of his chin, up to his left ear. His eyes held an ever-present solemnity. That sad and pretty face watching her with notes of embarrassment.

"He needed help," Brenner said nodding past her.

Ella nodded. "Nice music."

He snorted. "Drowns him out. I didn't go in!" Brenner said suddenly, as if this were a very important detail to add. "We didn't talk."

Ella glanced towards the door to Mr. Gunn's home. "Oh... Sorry."

"No. No, I meant... whatever. What's up, Ella?"

"I... Do you..." she hesitated, unsure how to even begin this conversation.

But Brenner seemed to misinterpret her muttering. He pointed at the trash. "Neighbors were complaining. Three weeks now." He shrugged, nodding towards the small trailer next to his father's. "The Martins were always kind to... mom." He frowned. "What's up?"

She stared at him. Brenner had a way of being brutally honest that often unnerved her. Ella didn't consider her feelings things to be often shared. Or even much acknowledged. But Brenner lived a life completely different than hers.

Manners, decorum, polite acquiescence and gentle answers made up most of Ella's preferred interactions.

Brenner on the other hand had a scorching tongue and a black-and-white way of viewing the world that she found both intimidating and challenging.

"I... need a babysitter."

"What?"

"I mean... another person to come with."

"Where?"

"That's... yeah. That's the problem. Helicopter."

"Where to?"

"Parcel. Heard of it?"

"Nope."

Ella winced. Brenner was still watching her closely, his face still somewhat flushed. She knew by coming here to speak with him, she'd cornered him on home turf while he was still in a vulnerable position.

She hadn't wanted to upset him, but she also knew that sojourning off alone with Mortimer Graves was a good way to get herself killed.

She still didn't know if what she was doing was the stupidest thing an agent had ever signed up for.

Or perhaps, worse, *she did know.*

So why had she come to Brenner?

"You're good with your gun," she said simply. "And... and you know... Navy and all that."

"You need a bodyguard."

"I guess so."

"Why? What's the job?"

"Apparently there have been a slew of disappearances in this small mountain town called Parcel."

"This town nearby?" He frowned, rubbing his hands against the back of his pants.

Ella winced, and began moving towards her vehicle, nodding as she did. She reached into the front seat and procured a bottle of hand sanitizer which she extended to him. He accepted it, pouring the contents into his palms and rubbing slowly.

The pungent, clean odor lingered.

"About a hundred miles north," Ella said. "In a valley. I looked it up—most maps don't list it."

"Huh. How come I haven't heard of it."

"Soney Dawkins' Cult," she replied.

"Oh, shit, *those guys*? So you're one of those soft-landing theorists, huh? Me too."

"No... I just... I don't think that plane crashed. What was it, like twenty years, right... Some say that community sprang up from it."

"Either way, why are you tangling with those quacks?"

She sighed. "Because... I have reason to believe young women have been going missing."

"Says who?"

"I..." Ella frowned. She couldn't exactly tell him the source. It didn't help that she didn't know *how* Graves was getting his information. So instead she said, "One-woman field office. I'd feel better if I had some backup."

"Why not a cop?" Brenner's eyebrows flicked up.

She studied him, then shrugged. "I guess you're right." She turned, slipping back into the car.

Brenner tossed the hand sanitizer through the open door before she could catch it. The bottle bounced off the front seat, hit the side door, then fell into the slot by the window. Brenner said, "Fine. I'll come. Are you paying?"

Ella shook her head. She winced. *Why* had she come to Brenner Gunn? Chief Baker was supposed to be her correspondent in Nome. Local police. But no... no, things with Baker were still strained. Ella still wasn't sure who had sent that assassin she'd found in her room.

No... that was why she'd come to Gunn. She could trust him. She nodded, reaching for the sanitizer to place it back in the appropriate slot in the dash.

Brenner called through the window. "Just let me grab the recycling. I'll be right there."

She nodded, watching as he strode back towards the waiting bins. As he did, he preferred his left leg. His right occasionally limped—an old injury. She wasn't sure if it was from his time as a mechanic, his tours in the Navy, or while working as one of the few U.S. Marshals in Alaska.

Either way, her eyes fell to the gun in Brenner's holster. She'd never seen someone nearly as fast on the draw or as accurate in high-pressure situations.

She swallowed slowly, wondering if she was being unkind to her old friend, dragging him into harm's way.

Then again, the previous day he'd jumped off a cliff to help her.

If there was one person she trusted to have her back, it was the limping man with the sad eyes.

Chapter 4

They had switched to Brenner's vehicle. In part, because he'd insisted, but also in part, because Ella didn't want anyone to track the onboard GPS of her field office's only vehicle.

This job was going to be completely off the books up until the point she wrote her field report.

Now, Brenner guided his old truck through the open gate of the small airfield. The staccato *thump* of helicopter blades against the cold wind under the sun began to pick up the closer they got.

Brenner gave a low whistle. "That's not a bird from this airfield. Shit—who's is that?"

Ella was also staring at the helicopter. A sleek, expensive-looking thing. And sitting in the front, in the pilot's chair, hands on the controls was a smiling, middle-aged man in a suit. He raised a hand, waving briefly at them through the glass.

"I... I don't know," Ella said if only to provide a non-answer.

"Who's the pilot?"

"Oh... you know."

"Nope."

"He's an old FBI friend."

"An agent?"

"NO!"

"Sheesh—no need to yell. What?"

"Just... a consultant. A CI."

"Ah... Gotcha. So he's your tip for Parcel? Why not just tell me?" Brenner gave her a sidelong glance, wrinkling his nose. He shook his head then parked the vehicle before slipping out the front seat and dusting his hands off on the back of his jeans.

Ella followed close behind.

The two of them reached the helicopter and Ella winced, gritting her teeth against the steady *thump* of the blades. She slipped into the front seat, though, the idea of entering the compartment so close to Mr. Graves made her skin crawl.

But in for a penny, in for a pound. She'd come this far...

Brenner slipped in behind them, expertly managing the sliding door, the seatbelts, the close proximity of the cramped space. He clearly knew his way around helicopters, already pulling on a headset.

Ella's own headset was handed to her by Graves. She accepted it, cautiously, and placed the headphones on. The sound of the whirling blades diminished a bit, replaced by a quiet radio crackle. Then a cheerful voice. "Hello, you two."

"Hey yourself," came Brenner's voice. "I'm Brenner. US marshal."

"Graves, a friend of Eleanor's."

"Yeah, she told me. CI, right? From the lower-forty-eight?"

The man chuckled. "I'm assuming you mean the lower states? No. I'm from across the pond."

Brenner nodded, flashing a thumbs up. Ella winced, feeling wrong in all sorts of ways. Just hearing the two men talk made her gut twist. It was like introducing her past to her darkest secret, and she was already beginning to regret the choices that had led her to this horrible moment.

But what else could she do?

Too much was at stake. Twenty dead women. Was he right? She'd already made her choice, after all. The radio crackle paused, then continued. "Hang on you two. We're leaving quick—pre-cleared. Should only be a couple hours to the town. Some water is in the back. Snacks under the tread."

Brenner instantly knew where to look and withdrew a pack of peanuts. He offered them to Ella, but she gave a quick, concerned shake of her head.

"Where did you know Ella from, again, Mr. Gunn?" said Graves conversationally.

"Nowhere," Ella snapped quickly. "Let's leave personal questions out of it."

Brenner shot her a curious look. Graves just smiled. "Professional it is, then. Just making conversation, Eleanor. Right—ready?"

Ella nodded this time as well. As she did, her phone buzzed. She frowned, glancing down. A small file had been sent to her inbox from an unknown number. "What is this?" she murmured.

"What? Oh—hmm. My contact must have sent you the information. That's the most recent missing person."

"Your contact? A friend of yours that so happens to know about this town?"

He winked. "We're keeping our pasts quiet, I thought."

Ella shook her head, glancing at the file, then opening it. She allowed her virus scanner to double-check; no ransomware or spyware was hidden, and then she opened the file.

A young woman's smiling face stared back.

Twenty-one-years-old, taking a gap year before finishing her final year of college judging by a statement transcribed from the mother. Ella frowned. The file wasn't formatted like something from law enforcement. A private investigator?

Judging by the helicopter and Mortimer's suit and cuff-links, she was starting to wonder if the Graveyard Killer also happened to be filthy rich.

"Rose Lewis," Graves said quietly. "Her mother hasn't heard from her in three days."

Brenner scowled, leaning back now, munching on his snack. "Let's go find her then."

"Yes, Mr. Gunn. I admire your gumption. Off we go!"

As the helicopter slowly lifted, Ella frowned.

Brenner hadn't given his last name.

So how had he known it?

The helicopter continued to lift, responding to the deft motions of its pilot, elevating over the metal fence, over the town of Nome—which sprawled along the coast below them—and then across the skyline, heading north into wilder, untamed parts of Alaska. Ella sighed, glancing once more down at the phone, studying the pleasant, smiling face of their missing person.

According to Graves, twenty other women had gone missing in the hidden unmapped town of Parcel. Maybe Graves was mistaken...

Maybe, she hoped, they'd find the missing persons alive and well.

But in her experience, wherever the Graveyard Killer showed up, bodies both preceded... and followed.

***

The man tossed another rock down the well, pausing to inhale slowly and stretch his arms. He massaged at the base of his neck then peered over the edge of the well, wincing. His fingers lowered, bracing against the stone, preventing him from tipping over and stumbling into the gullet of the dark watering hole.

As he frowned, peering at the work of his hands, he paused, listening.

A distant, strange sound. He turned slowly, looking up at the sky, his eyes narrowing. Was that...

A sleek, black helicopter cut above the trees, moving towards the lilac clearing. He frowned now, staring. The scent of warm air coming from the hot springs lingered. Another worse scent arose from inside the well.

He absentmindedly stooped, snatched another rock from his wheel-barrow and tossed it into the well.

It didn't splash.

He frowned out at the descending helicopter, watching as it veered over the small, idyllic lakeside town and then dropped towards the ground. The helicopter blades continued to whir as it descended, shielded from harsher winds by the backdrop of the mountains.

"Helen!" he called out, his voice tinged with concern. "Helen—any new supply drops due this week?" He waited, listening for the response from the open porch.

The front door was wide. People in town rarely locked their homes. It was a safe place. A quiet place. Crime was nonexistent.

A voice called out. "No—not until Sunday!"

He sighed, frowning and shaking his head, muttering to himself. He tossed another few stones down the well. Why was it that *he* always cleaned up other people's messes? Why was he the one who had to think like an outsider?

He grumbled to himself, dumping the last of the wheelbarrow's contents into the well, then snatching a bag of white powder, tipping and allowing it to pour into the stony gullet as well. All the while, his mood only darkened further.

People didn't understand what it took to shelter four hundred humans from harm. The families, the close-knit brothers and sisters in the village all depended on the elders to keep them safe.

And the elders?

They depended on him to clean up.

He dusted his hands off on the back of his overalls. Calling out, "Helen—gonna head into town, dear."

"Going to. Not gonna. We are not neanderthals in this household! You've been spending too much time with Jasper!"

He shook his head, muttering darkly, but then turning away from the well, grabbing the handles of the wheelbarrow and beginning to push it ahead of him, trundling the thing down the garden path, between the tomatoes rising up the wooden stems, the low ground clover and the small bean sprouts. Not much grew in winter in Alaska. But Parcel wasn't like the rest of the land.

Their mountains, their valley, their fertile soil, sometimes helped by the fertilizer their own animals provided or that supply drops brought in with a helping hand.

The mayor kept things running. The elders kept people safe.

And he kept things clean.

It was a well-oiled machine, but outsiders? They were like a wrench in the cogs.

He shook his head, strolling down the path, whistling as he did, wheel-barrow trundling. As he walked, he heard the sound of screaming suddenly erupt behind him from the direction of their log house. Painful, desperate, grunting yells. "Please! Please, I didn't mean to! Please!"

He shook his head, rolling his eyes. "Helen!" he called, pausing on the garden path and wiping the sweat from his brow. "Hey—*Helen!*"

The screaming, pained voice faded. A smiling, round face with a white bonnet poked out from behind the open log-cabin door. "Yes, dear?" she said.

He winced at her, then waved off towards the lilac field. "Outsiders," he said simply. "Better keep things down in there." The man's wife smiled, nodding quickly. She reached out a pudgy hand, portions of her fingers stained red.

His wife resembled a plump, pleasant homemaker. Some wives were often found covered in flour from making biscuits. Still others in streaks of mud or crayon from playing with their children. His own wife, though?

She'd been assigned a similar job to his. Clean up... after a fashion. And her black apron was stained in streaks of red. The carving knife clutched in her right hand was dripping on the black bag they'd placed over the welcome mat.

His wife never complained though. She gave a little wave to her husband and closed the door behind her.

A few seconds later, the screaming and begging started again. He shook his head. More messes to clean up.

But everyone had their role to play.

And his family's role was a very, very special one.

He continued pushing the wheelbarrow ahead of him, whistling as he did.

Chapter 5

The helicopter blades stalled above them, and Ella pushed open the door, hopping out onto the grass. She stared at their surroundings, stunned and more than a little confused.

"This... this isn't... what is this?" she asked, frowning and looking around.

The constant hum of the engines, the buzz from the radio, had left her with an itch in her head, but now, standing next to the suddenly silent machine, the quiet melded with the comforting scent of the purple flowers covering the grass and surrounding the clearing.

Brenner hopped out as well, whistling. "Nice place," he said. "Damn. Almost no snow."

She nodded slowly, glancing up at the large mountains circling the northern valley. She faintly detected an odd, freshwater scent she wasn't familiar with, but off to her right, near the base of one of the mountains she spotted steam rising from the ground. Hot water? Saunas?

Stranger still.

Flowers grew across the valley, extending towards clusters of *ancient* trees, rising from the dirt. The roots of the trees were larger even than Brenner himself, visible like humps descending from the base of the monstrous things into the ground.

The scent of the flowers and the warm freshwater also mingled with the fragrance of branches, leaves and the lake.

The lake itself occupied the heart of the tree groves. A pristine, glassy thing. At least fifty acres, likely larger. Wooden cabins lined the lake with privacy between them. Acres spread around the cabins, giving the various homes their own gardens and plots of land. All the homes were wooden with scant stone. Matching and tasteful, as if coordinated by some homeowner's association.

A much larger building—three stories with a dirt parking lot—was closest to them, at the end of a trail, about half a mile from the clearing. The window stood tall, outlined against the lake itself with a single bell in the tower. But a large sign over a green awning was difficult to read from this distance but gave the shop the appearance of some general store or grocery market.

A few small boats were floating on the lake. And still others were being set to water from launching zones on the shore. Very few cars visible. Very few engines or machines. Multiple solar panels were visible, hidden tastefully by brackets that made them look almost woodsy in nature.

The warm sunlight above assuaged Ella, comforting her, as if letting her know everything would be okay. The scent, the sights, the pristine beauty of it all, almost put her off guard.

Almost.

The sound of boots behind her, though, helped to remind Ella why they were here.

She shot a quick glance towards Mortimer and frowned as he strolled towards them, adjusting his suit again. The serial killer nodded politely at her, at Brenner, and then glanced at the town. "Quaint," he said simply before moving towards the three-story wooden structure with the dirt parking lot.

"Hang on!" Ella protested, hastening to keep up. She didn't snatch at him, though, again remembering how he could get when people threatened him physically.

Brenner strolled along at her side, watching everything with a curious expression. "Nice place..." he said. "I could live here."

"Unlikely," said Mr. Graves, shooting him a look. He then held up a placating hand towards Ella, still strolling ahead. "We're here to do it your way, yes?"

Ella blushed, shooting a quick glance towards Brenner then back. "By the book, yes. Like the last time you consulted on a case," she said, emphasizing the words through gritted teeth.

He just studied her, amused. "Quite."

"So we're here over a missing girl. Multiple missing girls, right?" Brenner said, frowning. "If the Dawkins cult moved up here, then we have our work cut out."

But Ella shook her head. "It's not the whole town. Only portions. Some are Dawkins, others are just... residents."

"Damn. Shit," said Brenner, frowning. "So we've got a wolves in sheep's clothing situation going on here."

Mortimer paused, his cuff-links flashing as he raised a hand. "Apologies," he murmured. "But the *Dawkins cult*?"

Ella nodded, scowling. "Yeah. Was this whole big thing about twenty years ago. When Brenner and I were still..." she trailed off, frowning, realizing she was revealing personal information. So instead, she said, "Twenty years ago, sixty-five people boarded a flight from Arizona. A private plane—no permissions. No licensing. They flew through federal airspace and were nearly shot down. They came out here... For five years, people thought they'd crashed. But then whispers and murmurs of the sixty-five passengers starting up their own little colony reached some of the coastal towns. We heard about them in Nome."

"So you think these folks are the Dawkins cult. Why the name?"

"That's what the pilot kept saying," Brenner answered. "When asked to identify himself. He just called himself Dawkins. Kept saying they were following the sun because it was the will of the oaks."

"The will of the oaks?" Mortimer said, blinking.

Brenner nodded, whistling and whirling a finger around next to his ear. "Yup. Dawkins cult. Harmless... So we thought. No one cared, anyhow. They kept to themselves. To be honest, I had no clue they were still up this way."

"We don't know they are," Ella replied quickly. "But an online search suggested that their plane's trajectory did come this way. The crash was estimated within fifty miles of here." She shrugged. "Strange place, strange town... missing people. It fits."

"Well then," said Brenner. "Nice and creepy. There may or may not be members of a cult living here... And we've got missing people. You don't... don't think they're *eating* the people do you?"

"Disgusting, Mr. Gunn," said Mortimer, wrinkling his nose. "I truly must protest—and in the presence of a lady, sir? Unbecoming." He marched ahead of them.

Brenner shrugged sheepishly, wincing apologetically at Ella.

She tried to smile, but it didn't reach her eyes. She frowned after Mortimer. The things *he'd* done to his victims were far worse than anything Brenner had whispered. It took a lot of gall to give Brenner a tongue-lashing over an errant question.

She frowned as she moved along, now within sight of the three-story structure which was, indeed, simply called *Hal's General Goods*.

As they approached the front door, Brenner leaned in, murmuring. "How do you know this guy again?"

Ella shook her head. "I don't. I barely do. He... he used to be a CI."

"Confidential informants aren't usually flying luxury helicopters, Ella."

She just shook her head, and took a few steps past the men, up the wooden stairs—which were built sturdy—and rapped her knuckles against the front door. Then, realizing it was a place of business, she winced sheepishly and pushed the door open with her shoulder.

A small, brass bell jangled overhead, and she entered the general store, looking about. Mortimer had been clear—he didn't know *who* was behind the disappearances. He hadn't said *how* he knew anyone had vanished. All he'd provided was a face, a name, and a story of others missing.

The same face which was now conjured in Ella's mind. She'd inherited the trait from her father. The ability to remember names and faces.

Rose Lewis. Twenty one-years-old. Gap year. The dusty shelves carried snacks, jerky, and a whole bunch of homemade jellies with tin lids. The jellies were labeled with paper and tape, each one boasting a name like *Roxanne, Helen, Wilma,* and *Maggie.* The flavors weren't mentioned at all, but Ella wondered if the townsfolk simply knew what they were getting based on the name of the jam-maker.

The jerky, she realized, was also homemade. But these had labels like, *Pete's Spicy Elk.* Or *Hal's Homemade Venison.* And one simply marked, *Extra Spicy Biltong (Matt's Peri Peri).*

There were wooden carvings on one wall and pottery on another, displaying vibrant colors like the mountain flowers and cute paintings of the very mountains they'd just crossed over as well as the lake now visible through the dusty, glass windows set in the opposite wall. Beaded necklaces dangled from a wired rack covered in hand-drawn postcards. Ella was impressed by the quality of the artwork.

A small clock above an old-fashioned cash-register ticked away, displaying a glass frame, but a metal face behind the glass displayed two bears crawling over a log, etched in copper.

Next to the register, large jars contained all manner of sweets. Stick candy, old-fashioned and of every flavor imaginable, like bubblegum, licorice, root beer, cherry, lemon and even rhubarb, and those were just the ones Ella spotted at a glance.

"Hey there, travelers!" a voice called from the back.

Ella watched as a straight-backed figure moved around from the back of the shop, approaching them. The man was dusting his hands off on a towel, flour falling as he did. The scent of warm, baking bread lingered from the back, and occasionally, Ella glimpsed a flicker of orange, suggesting a stone oven was in use.

The man had a friendly face and big, googly glasses that emphasized the color of his eyes, and he wore one of the beaded, blue and red necklaces available on the rack. He wore a loose, white shirt, but though the man looked to be middle-aged, he looked trim and very fit.

The man watched them from behind those glasses, still smiling congenially. "An absolute pleasure," he said, nodding at each in turn. "Welcome to Parcel. First time, guys?"

Ella began to reply, but Mortimer stepped forward, nodding politely and extending a hand, which the man behind the register accepted enthusiastically, pumping his arm up and down. "Dawson, by the way. Dawson Kinsey the third." He wiggled his eyebrows as if he'd just made a joke.

Ella blinked at the name. The candies. The warm bread. It all seemed a bit... too perfect.

"A pleasure to meet you, Mr. Kinsey," said Mortimer. "You may call me Graves." There wasn't even a hint of hesitation as he gave the fake name.

And if Kinsey detected an undercurrent, he didn't show it one inch. He continued pumping Mortimer's arm in greeting, smiling, his big eyes blinking behind those thick, googly glasses.

"And it is my first time," said Mortimer. "Thanks for asking."

"Oh well, sure. Shucks, we're nothing if not hospitable around here. We love outsiders." He beamed. "What can I do you for? Stick candy?" he tilted the licorice jar forward. A faint trail of flour fell on the counter, but he didn't notice.

Mortimer glanced down, pulled out a handkerchief, dusted the counter once, placed the lace back in his pocket and then looked up.

"I'm here to speak with my niece. You must have seen her recently. Rose Lewis."

The man behind the counter didn't blink, didn't falter. "Oh? Lewis? I thought you said your name was Graves."

"It's Graves Lewis."

Brenner shot him a look. Ella just watched. It was a heavier-handed approach than she might have used, but then again, it was *his* lead they were currently following anyway. So she just waited, watching.

In part, this was why she'd brought Brenner. In case Mortimer pissed anyone off so much that they had to come to the rescue.

Even the thought gave her pause and caused her heart to skip. She had brought her old friend, putting him in harm's way on a lead provided by a known serial killer who she had *witnessed* kill a man. He'd also disposed of the body from her motel by the time she'd returned.

Things were only going to get worse, and she had herself to blame for it.

Rose Lewis. She reminded herself. Rose Lewis. And at least nineteen others according to Mortimer Graves. And as much as he gave her the creeps, she couldn't say quite why, but she believed him.

She only hoped she wouldn't rue that tentatively placed, and very limited, trust.

"So you haven't?" said Mortimer.

"Seen her? No—the name doesn't ring any bells. We do have a bell, though—up in the tower. Want me to ring it for ya? Tourists love that." Mr. Kinsey grinned widely, all of his teeth visible. A few of the teeth were crooked, and none were nearly as white as Mortimer's. "Or, you know, you can check out Chester's tackle shop. Live bait. Couple'a canoes for rent. Fishing is great on the main lake."

"There's another lake?" Ella asked, leaning in.

"Huh? No. Just, you know—you can fish the lake."

"What's the steam at the mountains?" she said, fishing for different prey.

"Oh, we got some nice hot springs up this way. Runs through a lot of the area. Keeps things nice and toasty."

Ella nodded slowly. "I see. And is that available to tourists as well?"

"Sure, sure. Most things are. Just ask, you know." He chuckled. "Any of you want horseback rides? Maybe a carriage ride around the lake? You two look sweet together!"

Ella felt her stomach sink when she realized he meant her and Mortimer—the man was twenty years her elder, easy. Not to mention a prolific murderer.

Mortimer just grimaced, shaking his head. "No, no," he said, "My daughter and her boyfriend here are just looking for their cousin is all."

Ella scowled. She was certainly beginning to resent giving Mortimer the lead on this. Then again, she hadn't *given* anything, he'd simply taken it.

She heard a crackling sound and glanced back to see Brenner had helped himself to one of the *Peri Peri Biltong* snacks. Dried meat, by the look of it. And tasty by the look on Gunn's face.

"So you don't know of any tourists coming through recently?" Mortimer said casually, smiling politely. "She would have been twenty-one. Very friendly. A kind woman."

"No, mister, can't say I know anyone like that. My heartfelt condolences."

"Hmm? Why?" said Mortimer now, raising his eyebrows. "Condolences?"

"Umm, yeah. Because I can't help you. It hurts me to not help such lovely outsiders like yourselves. That's five dollars, mister, by the way. Or we take pelts, if you've got it." He glanced at their expressions then chuckled. "Just kidding about the pelts. Not the five dollars. Nope, sorry, no plastic. No reader. Just cash up here."

Brenner withdrew his offered card and pulled out a ten-dollar bill, shrugging. "You got change?"

"Afraid I don't, mister."

Brenner shrugged, snatched a second pack of the dried meat, and then looked out the window again at the pristine, clear lake. "Very nice place, this," he said. "Say, you don't know the name Dawkins, do you?"

The man behind the counter removed his glasses, rubbing them on his sleeve before returning them. "Huh, Dawkins? This a friend of your cousin's?"

"My—oh, uh, yeah."

"Nope. We have Naomi Dawson, but she lives in that house across the way—sells the finest kitchen sink cookies you ever done tasted. Mark my words—affordable too!"

Brenner gave a thin-lipped smile. Mortimer Graves wasn't smiling at all. And Ella felt as if she'd wandered from her normal life into the prelude of some horror movie. Things were too... quaint. Pretty, pleasant.

Unless of course, Mortimer was wrong about Rose Lewis. Maybe this town was just what it claimed to be. A Parcel in the barren wasteland. A home for weary travelers.

She glanced at the smiling store clerk. He seemed harmless enough. Healthy, vibrant, friendly. Nothing stood out to her. But in another way, she felt like a hound with its nose blocked. The scent of Mortimer Graves was a distracting one—not a literal scent. He was a hygienic man. But the man's very nature prevented Ella from focusing on the details here. To pick up on anything untoward.

Mortimer's own presence was such an alarming one that it masked any other warning signs.

Her stomach twisted as she watched the back of the man's head, wishing more than anything she had never met the Graveyard Killer.

Brenner was munching contentedly on his jerky, lingering behind her and watching. Mortimer tipped his head towards the clerk, then turned to glance at Ella. "Maybe a stroll around the lake?" he said conversationally.

"Aww, how sweet," Kinsey called out. "You sure you two ain't a couple? You don't look like kin. Don't worry, folk around here don't judge."

Ella stiffly shook her head. Mortimer just smiled again, but his hollow eyes carried no warmth. And Brenner frowned.

Mortimer began to brush past them, but this time, Ella moved ahead of him, determined not to be led by the murderer.

As they moved towards the door, Brenner said. "Any idea where a young woman might stay? Hotels, motels?"

Ella winced. A good question. She wasn't focused. She'd known it, and this proved it.

But the shop clerk said. "Only one motel in the place. Not really that, but the guest house behind Mrs. Puzo's."

"And which one's hers," Brenner replied.

"That one—directly across, behind the big carving of that wolf."

"Got it. Thanks."

And then Ella pushed through the door, leading the two men back out into the idyllic lake town and around the trail, her eyes fixated on the large carving of the wolf and the house beyond.

Any lead would do.

As they moved, Mortimer kept his voice low. "Rose was here."

"You're sure?" Brenner said. "Mind sending me that file, Ella?"

"No," she said quickly. Then swallowed, stuttering. "Sorry, no data." *Plus,* she thought, *the format would be a dead giveaway. This was a private tip, not a federal one.* The less questions to answer, the better.

Mortimer just shrugged. "She *was* here. The person I hired to find her tracked her here."

Ella blinked. This was the most he'd revealed about his process to her yet. A private investigator? But if so, *why* had he been tracking Rose? Was... was he somehow involved?

Ella bit her lip in frustration, allowing the flare of pain along her mouth to help her refocus.

The three outsiders moved along the lake, and as they followed the shoreline, figures in boats or on porches or strolling along the dusty road all glanced their way. Eventually, they waved.

Eventually.

But first, they watched, suspicious, eyes narrowed, distrustful.

The waves came second. A camouflaging gesture...

Seven times this happened. Seven stares, flickering frowns which vanished, then friendly waves.

The part that bothered Ella most was how they each waved three times with their right hand then dropped it. As if they were running on autopilot Or... somehow worse... as if they'd been *taught* how to wave.

Three waves. A smile. Bingo.

By the seventh time, Ella's own smile felt as fake as theirs. But they had reached the shadow of the giant, carved wolf. Menacing fangs sprouted from behind curled lips. The large wooden sculpture ornamented the side of the lake. Water spilled from a brass tube out of the wolf's back—spraying back into the lake and making the wolf look, oddly, like some sort of whale with a blowhole.

Ella glanced at the wolf for a second, frowning, then shook her head, moving up the wooden steps in the side of the incline, towards the small house which the shopkeeper had labeled as the motel.

Chapter 6

The welcome they received in Mrs. Puzo's home was distinctly chillier than that from Mr. Kinsey.

This made sense to Ella. In a stage production, the best actors were put in the foreground. The worst were used as extras in the back.

Mrs. Puzo sat in a rocking chair on her porch, eyeing the three figures moving up towards her. Her house, a timber-beam, single-story cottage situated on a multi-acre lot. Behind the main home, a second, smaller cabin settled under a large tree, green boughs reaching up to the clouds. Ella glanced at the small house, responding to Mrs. Puzo's scowl with an unreadable expression.

She leaned in, whispering to the men, "Keep her distracted."

And then, she slipped off, making as if she was moving back down the trail towards the lake. Brenner frowned after her. Mortimer just waved at Mrs. Puzo.

Then, while the old lady in the rocking chair was distracted, Ella shot a quick look along the lake. A few others were still watching her. Most of them fishing from small, wooden boats. She forced a smile; moved casually, hands in her pockets; and circled a small grove of trees that led up the incline around the side of Puzo's home.

Shielded from the porch and then ducking behind the trees to block the view of the fishermen, Ella suddenly dropped low and moved along the side of the wooden cabin, towards the second home under the enormous tree.

"Oh, she has to use the facilities," Mortimer was saying conversationally. "And how are you doing, madame, on this fine day?"

Brenner said nothing.

Mrs. Puzo responded, but her voice was fainter and far less energized than the Graveyard Killer's. Every time Ella thought of the man whose lead she'd chosen to follow, the more her stomach twisted. If the higher-ups back in Virginia found out what she was up to, it wasn't just her job they'd take.

But her freedom. Her reputation. Everything.

She wondered what her *father* would do if he found out. Her old man had eyes and ears everywhere in town. The King of Nome liked to keep watch on his subjects.

As she shifted under a window, moving in the shadows, inhaling the scent of fresh earth and fallen leaves, she frowned.

Her father, Jameson Porter, was on the short list of people who might have hired a hitman to come after her. That was another score she'd have to settle when back in Nome. If he *had* tried to kill her, then it would give her the perfect opportunity to put him where he belonged—in jail.

She shook her head in frustration, moving quickly and scraping her feet every few seconds against the grass to dislodge damp leaves.

She reached the small wooden cabin under the large oak tree and paused. A quick glance over her shoulder verified she wasn't being watched. No sign of security cameras, either. Or other things... like internet. Cell phones. Cars.

She frowned but approached the front door of the small guest house that apparently served as the town's only "motel."

She reached for the door handle.

Locked.

She hesitated, feeling a sudden exhilaration. Locked doors in a place like this were a good sign. As good as locked lips.

She could still hear Mortimer and Mrs. Puzo in conversation. One thing could be said for Mr. Graves—he knew how to distract a person. She moved along the side of the small cabin now, glancing through the window above the front porch. Though to call it a porch was generous. Really, it was mostly a naked wooden rail, with nails tastefully hidden, and small, lacquered branches holding it up. The window, though, was hidden by a thick curtain.

Ella hopped the fence—once she'd tested it would hold her slight weight—then circled the side of the cabin.

She paused, frowning.

Mud beneath one of the windows. But something else caught her eye...

Footprints in the mud, leading away from the cabin. Only one set of footprints. Someone had jumped *from* the cabin but had never returned.

Strange.

Faint shivers clawed up her spine, and she paused, inhaling slowly, trying to suppress her anxiety. And as she so often did with emotions like anger, irritation or fury, she bottled it. She pushed it deep, allowing it to slip beneath the surface of gray waters that served as her subconscious. She allowed it to linger there, unseen, untended.

Eventually, it would itch—it would protest. It would threaten to burst.

But until then, she left it dormant. The fear turned to a strange numbness as she forced the thought from her mind, using her will, her focus, to zero in on the muddy footprints. Small feet.

Ella moved her shoe next to one of the tread marks.

Only half an inch larger than her own. A woman's feet.

Ella turned now, shooting another quick glance along the side of the cabin. Still, no one had spotted her. She then reached for the ledge of the window, her fingers shaking.

The wooden ledge splintered as she scrabbled for purchase, her fingers finding little of substance to cling to. The voices from the cabin were growing louder now, Brenner's voice now joining in.

"We'd love to see the side entrance!" Brenner was calling out. "Lead the way!"

"Shit," Ella muttered, struggling not to rip the mildewed wood as she pulled herself up. She wasn't the strongest when it came to field testing, but she was also quite small and light. So with some effort, she managed to muscle her way up to the ledge eight feet off the ground. The window settled high in the wall, far above where anyone might peer through accidentally.

Now, her face pressed against the glass and her cheek to the cold glaze. Off to her left, around the side of the main cabin, she watched as an older woman in a shawl tottered forward, her curved, wooden cane tapping against the ground as she gestured with spindly fingers for two unseen shadows to follow.

Brenner was still speaking, loudly. Mortimer had gone quiet.

Ella, wondering what the hell she'd gotten herself into, breathed desperately, slipped her finger under the window and pulled.

Like she'd suspected, the muddy footsteps *leaving* the cabin suggested someone had used the window as an egress. And it also suggested they'd left it open.

So the window scraped up. Ella gasped.

Mrs. Puzo began glancing up and over, her wrinkled features like those of a bulldog. Brenner suddenly spotted Ella, his eyes widening briefly. But then he leaned in, pressing his hand on the motel-keeper's shoulder. "Sorry!" he apologized as he nearly tripped.

Mrs. Puzo didn't seem to mind the touch of the tall, handsome man. But she did hesitate, glancing at him, giving Ella enough time to wiggle through the open window, her belly scraping against the splintered, soggy ledge.

She let out a desperate gasp as she *thumped* onto a wooden floor inside the room, then hastily reached up and back, still kneeling on the ground, pulling the window closed.

It was only as she paused there, leaning against the wall and breathing heavily that she realized if footprints had formed in the mud, her *own* footprints might be easily visible.

She winced, tensing and peering through the glass out onto the ground. But no figures approached. The mud was clear. She stared, waiting. But by the sound of things, Mrs. Puzo was taking them around the side of the main house, leading them away, once again, from the cabin.

Ella leaned back, her shoulders brushing against the wall. She exhaled slowly, allowing her pounding heart to settle.

And then she looked around the cabin.

A small, cramped space. Not nearly as dusty as the windows had been and mostly untouched by sunlight since the curtains were thick and the window Ella had come through faced thick trees with similarly dense branches intercepting the beams of the star.

She straightened slowly, dusting herself off, ears perked in case anyone approached, but for the moment feeling very much alone.

She glanced off towards the bed in one corner. A squat, four-legged hand-made wooden frame with a soft cot. The pillows were lumpy but looked soft—hand-stitched too, judging by the occasional gap in the threading.

Ella always did have an eye for details, but the small cabin serving as the town's only motel didn't offer much in the way of evidence.

And evidence of *what*?

Mortimer had said a girl was missing. Had said many others had gone missing... And she believed him. She couldn't say *why* she believed him though, she'd only met him once before. She frowned, the floor creaking softly as she approached the bed, studying it.

She leaned down, her hand braced against the cot—it had bounce, as if instead of springs in it were simply made of sponge.

71

She glanced under the four-poster elevated space, studying the dark recesses. No sign of anything except some dust.

She shook her head, withdrawing and glancing towards a small cupboard, a miniature coffee table with an outdated sports magazine from the 90s by the look of it. And a record player set on a cabinet filled with vinyl.

She approached the cupboard, opening a drawer. A few plastic utensils. A wooden bowl—hand hewed. She frowned, looking around the place. Footsteps leading away... but nothing in the cabin.

And no returning footsteps.

"Curious," she murmured aloud.

She checked the rest of the cupboard but came up empty then approached the vinyl player. She scanned through the cabinet of albums, hesitating occasionally. Most of them were covered in dust, even some cobwebs, suggesting the record player didn't get much use.

But she paused. To the left, three of the records were less dusty and held no cobwebs. She pulled them out, studying them. Bands she didn't recognize. Names that meant nothing to her. Snow something. Purple Plums. She didn't even read the name of the last one, because something else caught her attention.

There, wedged in against the record... a small folded note.

She stared, and then pulled it out, her fingers shaking.

She unfolded the note hastily, studying it with a tremor of excitement. And then she began to read, cautiously. Only a few lines of hastily scribbled text, and a couple of hearts drawn in blue ink on the yellow, lined paper.

The note read: *Can't stop thinking of you... I miss you already. If mom finds out though, we're both in real trouble. Don't let the elders know. See you tonight. Much love. A.*

She read it again, frowning. Who was A? And who was the letter addressed to?

She glanced at the empty bed. No sheets either. No bedding besides the pillow. Nothing in the small, copper sink. No toilet on the premises, suggesting there was likely an outhouse.

She frowned towards the door, hesitant. It was closed shut, sturdy enough. She glanced at the window.

So why had someone gone out the window? And what did this letter mean? *Don't let the elders know.* What did that *mean*? Elders? Like in a church? She hadn't seen any church buildings among the cabins... If not a church, then what if it was something far more unusual?

She thought of the so-called Dawkins' cult...

But much of it was still conjecture. And there was no evidence the cult had been *violent.* Still...

She shook her head, slowly pocketing the note, closing the cabinet with the vinyl and glancing towards the window again.

She approached slowly, frowning into the dark, and staring out across the muddy terrain. The footprints reached a grassy area then disappeared. Footprints, though, that were heading in the exact opposite direction from the lake.

What was back that way? She hadn't spotted anything earlier.

She was getting ready to go, when something caught her attention.

There, on the ground, the faintest film of yellow sawdust.

The only issue was that the floorboards were brown—not light yellow. She stared, wrinkling her nose, then slowly tilted her head, glancing up at the ceiling.

An old, outdated fan was motionless, but the blades were devoid of dust, suggesting it had seen recent use.

But there, a few feet away from the edge of the fan... She frowned, rising on her tiptoes.

An outline in the wood.

Barely visible. She hardly would have noticed if not for how dark the room was, save the faint illumination coming through the window, catching the outline just-so.

She felt a faint shiver, though she couldn't say why. It took her a few seconds to consider her options. She paused, listening for noise in the distance, but there was still no sound of voices. The men were distracting the motel lady for a bit longer.

She pulled the coffee table over, stepped on it, once she'd tested it was sturdy enough, and then—using the boost in height from the table—reached up and poked her fingers against the rectangular outline in the ceiling.

The moment she did, there was a soft *click,* and a trapdoor slowly opened with a silent swish, suggesting it moved on greased, well-oiled hinges. Her eyes widened as she stared at the trapdoor, stunned.

"What the hell..." Her voice whispered in the room, a faint breezy murmur of surprise.

She wrinkled her nose, shot a look to the window off to her left, and then reached up, pulling the trapdoor fully open.

With that same prickle along her spine spreading, she pulled herself up the small, dangling wooden ladder, into the attic—which certainly hadn't been apparent from the outside. A hidden room above the motel.

She poked her head through, feeling a rising sense of unease. As she did, blinking a few times in the dark space, she began to rotate her head, slowly, peering out at rafters and flat plywood platforms.

And then came the *creak.*

She froze. A sudden sound behind her. She whirled, nearly falling.

And then a raccoon darted into a gap under two of the beams, disappearing. She exhaled desperately, her heart pounding wildly, and she nearly slipped from her purchase, her hands tight, knuckles white where they gripped the ladder. The fall from the base of the short ladder to the table was only a few feet, but if she fell funny, she could easily break a leg or sprain an ankle.

Explaining *that* to the town, to the motel lady, wouldn't be fun.

She paused for a moment, scanning the rest of the dark space.

And there, she spotted something disconcerting. A small, ratty blanket in one corner. A pillow on it. A pile of old magazines. And there, in the floor where the fan would have gone, concealed by the perforated metal ornamentation, was a peephole, visible now from the way the faint light shone into the dark through the gap.

The hole was right next to the blanket in the far corner. And... as she stared, Ella realized it overlooked the bed in the room below.

The shiver intensified.

The peephole stared directly down at the bed of any guest who came through. Her heart pounded horribly and she swallowed.

"What the actual fu—"

Thump. Thump. The sound of footsteps against stairs. Voices now, which had been faint and she'd failed to notice in her fright.

Ella suddenly cursed. Someone was coming to the door of the cabin. She heard the sound of a lock. She knew she could hide in the attic, but something told her this was a bad decision.

Perhaps it was simply the creepy nature of the place or the prickles still pawing at her spine.

Whatever the case, she dropped onto the coffee table with a nimble *thump*. She reached up, closing the trap door. She hopped off.

The locks opened in the front door. She winced, cursing softly and pulled the coffee table back into place as best she could. No more time, though.

The door opened slowly. Voices echoed through. One of them Brenner's, urgent and attempting to distract.

But Mrs. Puzo was saying, "Now, now—I'm just checking to see if everything's clean. The room hasn't been stayed in for weeks—it's all yours, of course."

Ella was halfway to the window, she reached it, slid it up. The door opened.

Three figures were outlines. Two of them staring past the motel-keeper, both suddenly noticing where Ella was slipping through the side window.

Mrs. Puzo's torso faced the room, but her head was craned back, again her eyes fixated on Brenner as if delighted to watch him.

Mortimer just stared at Ella, those deep, dead, hollow eyes amused. She scrambled through the window, dropped and closed the window as softly as she could.

She thumped against the mud, breathing desperately.

And then a hand landed on her shoulder. "Hello there—I don't think we've met."

A yelp caught in her throat and she spun around, heart hammering in rapid tempo. She stared at the man facing her, and she went for her gun.

Chapter 7

Ella's palm froze, braced against her holster hidden by the hem of her secondhand sweater. She stared at the man facing her, her breath coming in slow gasps. He had white bandages across one side of his face, which had startled her at first.

He was a young man, perhaps only in his early twenties, and might even have been attractive if not for the bandages wrapped along his cheek, up past his ear and under his small, newsboy cap which angled off to the side.

He smiled sheepishly at her. "Sorry," he said. "Didn't mean to startle you." The smile, like the waves from the fishermen, looked rehearsed.

"Oh, yeah—no," Ella said, fumbling. "Just..." she looked up and down. "Was just testing out the room, you know. Fire hazard."

He watched her. His hair was even more pale than hers—instead of blonde, his was nearly white. His features carried a similar pallor, but this looked like a function of something else... Fear? Blood loss?

She couldn't be sure.

He winced, touching gingerly at the side of his face, then murmured, "You probably shouldn't be back—"

"Abraham? Oh—and... There you are! What are you two doing back here?"

Ella and the young man named Abraham both turned sharply to face Mrs. Puzo and her two hangers-on.

Ella tensed, looking anywhere but up at the window, frozen in place and shifting her posture. She felt the way the mud gave out under her feet and tensed.

Abraham stepped forward, rubbing at the side of his face. "Hello, Mrs. Puzo," he said politely, nodding his head, but then wincing, his fingers darting to touch delicately at the side of his face.

"Abraham," she replied, watching him closely.

The two locals fixated on one another, silent and quiet, neither looking away. Briefly, it almost felt as if they shared an unspoken conversation. Ella's mind scrambled, her hand still rested on her sweater against her holster.

The note crinkled in her pocket as she shifted, and another thought occurred to her.

A.

Abraham?

The young man coughed delicately and said, "She was just admiring the cabin," he said, nodding at Ella. He didn't look at the window, didn't mention it. In fact, as he stepped forward, she noticed the way he swept his foot along the mud as if intentionally clearing the tracks.

Ella kept her expression polite, but it naturally wanted to turn into a frown.

The two men flanking Mrs. Puzo were both watching quietly. Brenner, seeming to sense the tension of the moment, as well as the unspoken words exchanged between the two locals, said, "Don't mean to interrupt, but we were hoping to find a place for the evening."

She glanced at him now, frowning hesitantly. "It's not late yet," she said softly. "Give me some time to clean—you saw the state of the place."

"It looked wonderful to me," replied Mortimer.

"It needs cleaning," she replied sharply. And a bit of the grandmotherly expression faded to one of disapproval. This same frown turned to Abraham. "We like things clean around Parcel, don't we, Abe?"

"Yes, ma'am."

"And I'm sure you learned your lesson, yes?"

He wagged his head up and down, occasionally scratching at his head wrap but doing his best, it seemed, to remain docile.

Again, Ella felt a strange shiver along her back. Nothing was adding up. She vaguely thought of her sister Cilla. Priscilla was the sort who wouldn't function in a town like this at all, where every second glance and every subtlety was more honest than the words and smiles.

Ella tried not to roll her eyes thinking of her sister. If anything, Priscilla would burn the whole place down just to get some answers. Her sister wasn't exactly the subtle sort.

The young man was moving off now, taking his chance to slip away while he was no longer being questioned. As he left, though, Ella watched as he meticulously stepped on the mysterious trail of footprints leading from the window, covering them with his own. Ella's own footprints were left untouched.

He glanced back and winced when he realized Ella was staring directly at him. A panicked look crossed his eyes, and his pale, blonde hair fluttered as he brushed it back beneath his newsboy cap.

Ella held his gaze for a moment, glanced at his feet, up again and winked. He exhaled slowly, some of the fear in his eyes fading to be replaced by relief.

But Ella had a hunch. And with her back turned to Mrs. Puzo, Ella slowly reached into her pocket and withdrew the crumpled note. She unfurled it slowly, pressed against her sweater front, so no one but Abe could see.

As it unfolded, and she smoothed it out, he stared, his eyes bugging.

He didn't look away.

She raised a questioning eyebrow—he swallowed, stuttered something incoherent, then turned and disappeared through the trees, moving rapidly around the edge of the lake.

Ella was tempted to go after him but decided this would only draw unwanted attention. So instead, she placed the note back in her pocket and faced Mrs. Puzo and her two companions.

The woman was saying, "Later this evening. For now, why don't you check out the bait shop? Rent a boat. Enjoy yourselves. We also have some nice restaurants along Hedge Creek.

"I can't say we're particularly hungry just yet," replied Mortimer conversationally. He opened his mouth to add more, but Ella raised her hand, clearing her throat. "Actually, we are hungry. Let's go get a bite."

The two men glanced at her, frowning. But she jerked her head to the side when Puzo wasn't looking, and they both went quiet, allowing her to march past them.

"Wait!" the motel-lady said suddenly.

Ella froze, glancing back. She felt her heart skip as Puzo was glancing up at the window Ella had used. The woman paused, turned. She then pointed. "There's only one bed in there. And this is an old-fashioned sort of place."

Mortimer said quickly, "These two are married. She's my daughter. I'll sleep on a couch if you have it."

Puzo nodded approvingly. "A couch we have. Come back this evening—the room will be ready. That's five hundred for the night, by the way. Cash."

Brenner whistled softly. "Lotta money, that."

But Mortimer didn't even blink. "Easy enough. Here—up front payment. Consider the room reserved." He pulled a sleek, black wallet from his suit pocket, extracted five crisp bills hot off the press and handed them to the woman.

Then, while she was counting them, a look in her eyes of excitement, Ella gestured at the two men and hastened away.

Brenner and Mortimer fell into step, following her hastily down the trail back towards the lake. As they did, and once they were out of earshot, Ella murmured beneath her breath. "There's a hidden room above the bed."

"Pardon me?"

"A secret room, with a peephole. It's above the bed in a hidden attic."

Mortimer cleared his throat delicately. "Odd," he said.

"Perfect," Brenner replied. "This whole town gives me the creeps, but if someone's gonna try and sneak into that place and watch us, we can catch 'em." He shrugged. "No need to bait the hook if the fish are swimming straight into the boat."

Ella frowned at this troubling thought. In this analogy, she couldn't help but feel as if *they* were the bait. And the idea that someone might creep along in the ceiling above them, watching their every move only sent shivers and tingles along her back.

But Brenner had a point. If something was up in the town, if a killer was on the loose, then some creep in the attic would be a good start. Did Mrs. Puzo know about the hidden room?

"Another thing," Ella whispered. "We need to find that kid."

"Who?" Brenner shot back.

"The young guy. He's gotta be Rose's age. I found a letter in the cabin. It was signed *A.*"

"There are a lot of names that start with A," Mortimer said.

"Yeah, well... He didn't tell on me. Plus... his ear. That was weird, right? What was wrong with his ear?"

The two men didn't say anything at first. But Mortimer murmured. "He was terrified and in pain."

"Excuse me?" Brenner asked, shooting the man a sudden, questioning look.

Mortimer was looking straight ahead as the three of them kept their voices low and moved along the side of the lake. "I said," Mortimer murmured, "the young man was terrified. It's in the eyes. You can always see it if you look closely enough."

Ella hated how much Mortimer sounded like a wine-taster commenting on his favorite vintage.

Brenner was frowning now, though, he often scowled. Where Mortimer's eyes were hollow but his voice full of charisma, Brenner's eyes held a depth that often caused her heart to ache. But his voice was cold. At least, to most people.

But in recent days...

Ella wasn't sure. But Brenner seemed different to her. He'd told her something the previous day, while caught in a blizzard along the side of a cliff, trying to dry their clothes. Something she hadn't been able to question him about a second time.

Comments on their history together. Young love—just like the note seemed to hint at.

Ella sighed slowly, pushing the thoughts from her mind as best she could. She murmured, "We need to find Abe and talk to him. I think he might know something about Rose."

"You think Rose was in that cabin?" Mortimer said.

"I don't know. Someone was. Footprints—a woman's—leading away, not back. Puzo lied. She said no one was there in weeks, but the dust is gone. Someone's muddy prints led from there. I'd bet anything someone was sleeping there last night... at least, within the last couple nights."

"And you believe those were Rose Lewis's footprints?"

"Yeah, but Abe was wiping them away. He saw me watching him and looked embarrassed."

"Guilty or embarrassed," said Mortimer. "They often look the same."

"Both," she said. "That's why we need to talk to Abe."

"Chat with the blond weirdo and then sleep in a room while a creep watches us," said Brenner. "Sounds great. Thanks for inviting me along on this, Ella."

"Would you like to leave?" she said.

"No, I think I'll stick around..." As Brenner said it, his scowl fixated on Mortimer, watching the man from behind as the three of them moved up the lake trail. The serial killer didn't notice the look as he strode confidently forward, a few steps ahead.

But Brenner's glare carried every tone of suspicion Ella might have suspected. He was watching Mortimer like a hound eyeing a wolf through a fence. Confident that this creature, though it *resembled* something familiar, was a new type of threat entirely.

Ella kept her own expression a mask, the guilt in her gut growing.

Mortimer had promised not to harm their killer—to do things by the book. He was here as a confidential information, that was all. A CI. The FBI often worked with CIs, didn't they?

Yes... it was nothing too unusual. Besides...

Ella exhaled shakily... one thing at a time. "Did you ask Puzo about Rose?" she said.

"Never heard of her," Mortimer replied over his shoulder. "She was scared, though. Pretended to be angry, but she was scared."

"You seem pretty confident about everyone's feelings, guy," Brenner said. "You a shrink or something?"

Mortimer looked back, flashing his white teeth. "Or something. Ah—look, up ahead. Sheriff's office. If anyone can help us find that boy, perhaps fellow law enforcement, hmm?"

Without an ounce of shame or hesitation, the serial killer turned and marched confidently towards the sheriff's office, his arms swinging freely at his sides.

A few more people passed by, two carrying a canoe, and another with a basket over her arm. All three of them paused, frowned, then waved at the newcomers.

"Creepy as shit," Brenner said, not even bothering to keep his voice low as he passed the woman with the basket.

Her smile never faltered, her waving hand completed its three repetitions before dropping at her side.

Ella only felt the shivers along her spine increasing in intensity as she marched up the steps into the sheriff's office, following Mortimer, and pushed open the front door.

Chapter 8

Brenner stayed back, watching as the two others moved up the stairs, pushing through the door and entering the sheriff's office. He turned away, inhaling the scent of the lake, his eyes flicking from the water, to the buildings, to the bell tower across the lake.

If he was setting up surveillance, he'd avoid the bell tower. Too obvious. Some of the trees, though? Perfectly masked. Maybe in those thick branches, three-quarters of the way up.

His gaze took in every possibility, flitting from the trees back to the people.

Otherwise known as threats.

Something was off about Parcel. The Dawkins cult had always fascinated him as a kid. He'd long read articles about the stolen plane, the errant flight across the lower-forty-eight, and then the crash landing in Alaska.

At least, he'd been told they'd crashed. But according to Ella, *this* was within fifty miles of their supposed downfall.

It didn't mean much... But the people here were acting strange.

"Not as strange as you, though..." he muttered, staring through the glass door of the sheriff's office at the man named Mortimer Graves. A polite, posh, rich-as-hell fella. With *that* kinda money. The sort of money Brenner would never touch in his life.

He didn't mind. He knew enough people with money to think it did much beyond a certain level.

Hell, his ex-wife came from *that* kinda money, too.

Still, why was a prim billionaire with his own damn helicopter waltzing around with Eleanor Porter?

He didn't like it.

Didn't like the man, either. It was in the eyes. Something was missing. The same sorta something that the men Brenner often hunted had missing. As a marshal, he had the delightful task of finding fugitives or escorting prisoners. And more often than not, men who'd spent their lives so far outside the bounds that they ended up in maximum security facilities had the same look.

He didn't like the guy. Not one bit.

Still, he didn't strike Brenner as a threat to Ella. Not yet. Brenner knew a dangerous man when he spotted one, but the Brit seemed fond of Ella, in a weird way. CI, she'd said.

"Whatever..." he muttered, frowning and massaging at his leg.

He heard laughter from the lake and watched curiously as two men and two young women tried to launch their canoe. One of the men had fallen in the water, soaking himself. Cursing and spluttering, he rose to his feet, splashing in the shallows.

One of the girls, the one who'd waved at Brenner earlier, wasn't laughing. Her expression was silent, muted. Almost... scared? Nah. Brenner wasn't a shrink—he'd leave the guesswork to the CIs.

But the *other* young woman, the one who *hadn't* waved at him, nor even glanced at him earlier—which was why she'd stood out in a town like this—was pointing and laughing at the young man in the shallows. Her giggle was as crystal clear as the swirling water itself.

But the man wasn't laughing. His friend wasn't either. They both scowled at her, and Brenner watched in some curiosity.

"You think something's funny?" snapped the wet man, pointing at the laughing young woman. "Shut up!"

"Let it go, Larry," said the other girl, her expression still neutral.

"Yeah, Larry!" said the laughing one. "I'm just teasing. It was funny—I'm sorry. See, here, I'm not laughing anymore."

It was a good effort at least, but the woman was struggling to hold her amusement in check. This only irritated the man named Larry some more. "Cut it out! *Now*!" he snapped.

"Let it go," said Larry's friend. This second man, with a buzzed head was glancing towards Brenner and frowning. The shaved-headed one pulled at Larry's arm, muttering something. "We got company," he said.

Brenner's look of curiosity had disappeared now. He knew a punch before it went flying. And Larry's hand had curled into a fist.

Brenner slowly approached now, frowning at the four figures splashing in the shallows. He shot a quick look back towards the Sheriff's office, but no one called after him. Now, the sun caught the glass in such a way, it hid the silhouettes of his companions.

"You guys alright?" Brenner said conversationally, his fingers hooked into his belt.

The two men turned now, frowning. The laughing girl went quiet, wincing now, hesitant. "Are you a cop?" she said.

Brenner looked at her. "You're not from around here, huh?"

"Umm... N-no. Are you a cop, then? I—we have permits for the lake!"

But Brenner shook his head. "I'm just making conversation. What's your name?"

"Bronwyn," she said shakily. "W-why? What did I do?"

"Nothing. When did you get to Parcel?"

"She doesn't want to talk to you, man," Larry snapped, stepping forward. He was still dripping. His flannel sleeves both soaking wet. Larry stepped close, intending to force Brenner to step back.

But Brenner couldn't be bothered. He stood his ground and their chests bumped. Now, the bald guy was watching his friend. Larry was glaring at Brenner. The one girl, the local as Brenner pegged her, watched dispassionately. The other one looked frightened and excited at the same time.

"Where'd you pick her up?" Brenner said, nodding towards Bronwyn.

"How about from None-of-Your—"

"Right, I get it."

"—Business, that's what—wait, what?" Larry blinked, wrinkling his nose. It took him a second to figure out what had happened, but then abandoning the trail of thought, he just glared and bumped his chest against Brenner's again. "You should leave too, tourist."

"Hang on, now," said the girl who'd remained quiet up to this point. "Guests are all welcome. We're very hospitable in Parcel," she said, but it was with the conviction of a bad actor reading off a cue card.

Brenner briefly wondered what Ella might do in a situation like this. She'd likely apologize, step back and keep the peace, all the while smiling politely. And dishonestly.

Brenner wasn't much like Ella.

Instead of retreating, he glared, raised a jutting finger and snapped, "Bump me again, and I'll put your testicles in your stomach."

Larry blinked in surprise at the sudden aggression. He opened his mouth, closed it again, then his scowl twisted his features, and he took a threatening step forward. "You think you're tough?" Larry said, his voice low. He glanced nervously back and forth, then leaned in.

Brenner's hands tensed, but the gesture wasn't a violent one, though, it still brimmed with aggression as Larry whispered, "I know people. People around town... People you don't want to cross, man. So why don't you back the hell away, huh?"

And then, Larry gave Brenner a shove.

At least, he tried to. But the moment the young townie's hand touched Brenner's chest to push him, the ex-SEAL moved swiftly.

He snatched the wrist, twisted the hand and then resisted the urge to snap the bones. This was Brenner's version of restraint. He left the bones intact, and, still holding the twisted wrist, gave Larry a little push back towards his friend. "Watch your boy," said Brenner coldly. "Or he's going to get cracked."

But instead of holding his friend back, now the bald young man scowled, pushing away from their fishing vessel. And Brenner spotted pale fingers slipped into a hidden belt sheath and emerge with a small, scaling knife which glinted dully.

Brenner clicked his tongue, wrinkling his nose in disgust. "Seriously? I mean... *look* at it, don't you know how to take care of a blade? That's half rust."

Larry was wincing, massaging his arm. His friend held his knife tight. Bronwyn, the outsider, watched in horror, her laughter gone. The other young woman, the local, watched dispassionately, curious but disinterested as if it were all some big show.

A knife had appeared in Larry's hand now. Brenner glanced between the two young men, and only now did he take a step back. "Careful boys—let's not escalate things, here." And though he tried to keep his tone accommodating, Brenner's eyes must have betrayed his thoughts. His scowl flickered back and forth between the two of them.

And Larry, breathing heavily, snarled, "If you knew the folk I do, you'd be gone by now, stretch."

A few other fisherman on the lake were glancing over. One boat, with a green hull, carrying two fishermen, was coming their direction slowly, the two older men in the vessel frowning as they crossed the expansive waters.

Brenner pointed at each one in turn. "Either of you know a guy named Abe?" He shot a look towards the girls in the water, raising an eyebrow. In a town this small, there couldn't be *too* many Abraham's.

No one replied at first, but then, the tourist said, "Isn't that Helen's son? The one at the square dance last night?"

"Shut up, Bronwyn!" snapped Larry.

The other girl was shaking her head, muttering, "What did I say about bringing a tourist, huh? What did I say..." she murmured, quietly though, frowning.

The two men approaching in the green fishing boat were now picking up the pace, water expanding to white as they cut through the lake.

Larry and the skinhead, which to Brenner just sounded like a bad band name, hadn't noticed the approaching vessel. Or if they had, they simply didn't care. Now, both of them carrying blades, they took a step towards Brenner onto the shore.

"You sure?" Brenner said, tensed where he'd stepped back.

"Come on, gimp," snapped Larry. "I don't think you're so tou—"

He didn't finish, as Brenner hadn't stepped back to retreat, but rather to plant his off foot on sturdy ground. And then his left foot shot out like a whip. It connected with Larry's chin faster than he could raise his knife. The skinhead yelped and slashed, but Brenner dropped the leg and followed up with two quick blows with the flat of his palm.

In the Navy, they weren't taught to *control* or de-escalate. They were taught to subdue in whatever way possible.

And so Brenner didn't throw the punch with his full force, instead leaning back a bit and allowing the heel of his hand to connect.

Larry hit the ground with a *thump* from the head kick at the same time that Brenner's palm connected with the skinhead's neck.

The knife missed. The skinhead gasped, gurgled and stumbled back, splashing in the water.

Brenner rubbed his hand against his jeans, shaking his head in frustration. He glanced at the girl on the boat. "You should probably get out of town," he said with a shrug.

She stared at him, then at the two young men laying in the mud, then up again. "The next supply drop isn't for a few days!" she said with a squeak.

Brenner nodded slowly. "Where are you staying?"

Bronwyn blinked a few more times, hesitating. The second girl was still frowning, shaking her head, but had turned to watch the green boat with the outboard motor speeding towards them.

Bronwyn said, "The general store owner had a spare room. He's letting me stay there cheap."

Brenner nodded. "Probably lock the door. Here, carry this. Keep an eye out." He bent over, picked up the cleaner of the two knives from the mud, wiped it off on Larry's shirt where the man lay unconscious, then handed the weapon to the girl.

She stared at it before accepting, but then, with trembling fingers, took it. The mud stained her fingertips as she withdrew a still-trembling hand. "I.. I..." she didn't finish the sentence. Clearly both scared and confused.

Suddenly, a door opened, and a voice called out. "Sheriff's not in—Brenner? Where are—what the hell?"

He began to turn to glance in Ella's direction, but before he could, a voice suddenly echoed over the lake, coming from a megaphone, which crackled as it erupted with static and sound. "You on the shore, hands where I can see them. Hands where I can see them!"

The local girl who'd been muttering waved now, "Hey dad—this guy just kicked Larry in the face. Not really sure what happened to Reef."

The man on the boat with the megaphone frowned, approaching the shore, a gun raised. A second man behind him was busily stowing hooks in a tackle box. A couple of fishing poles braced in metal brackets were subsequently stowed along the side of the boat.

Both men wore flannel and jeans. But the one with the megaphone was holding up a badge, flashing it.

Brenner stood stock still, grimacing. He could hear Ella approaching from behind, accompanied by her strange companion. He also heard the door to the sheriff's office open again, suggesting a clerk or a secretary was now stepping out to watch the scene.

Brenner's eyes, though, were on the approaching sheriff.

The tourist, Bronwyn, stepped hastily up the shore, and as she passed Brenner, she muttered, "That's Sheriff McClellan. His family runs this town." Brenner noticed her tuck the knife in her belt, under her shirt hem. And then she set off, moving casually but quickly in the direction of the General store.

Brenner slowly raised his hands, waiting for the boat's prow to crunch up against the shore, furrowing mud. The two self-proclaimed law

98

enforcement officers in plain clothes hopped out. Guns pointed at Brenner.

Ella hurried down the steps, scowling. She'd been gone for two minutes. Two damn minutes and Brenner had laid out some of the locals.

She brushed past the tall marshal, raising her own badge and forcing a smile. "Are you Sheriff McClellan?" she called out, echoing the name the desk attendant had provided.

She stepped swiftly in front of Brenner.

Two guns were brandished in her face but dipped slowly as eyes fell on her badge. Brenner stood behind her and greeted the cops. "Hey there. What seems to be the problem?"

The second man in the boat, skinny and bald with a thick, lumberjack beard had dropped to the unconscious townie's side, patting his face. After a few seconds, the man in the mud groaned, blinked a few times then sat up.

The other man was holding his throat, wheezing and glaring daggers at Brenner. He kept pointing, trying to say something, then lowering his hand again as a new wave of gasping overtook him.

Ella glanced at them both, taking it all in quickly. She had spotted the knife Brenner handed to the girl who was retreating around the lake. She also spotted a far rustier knife laying on the ground next to the rousing townie.

She glanced at Brenner, who shrugged sheepishly, then back at the man with the upraised megaphone, the badge dangling from his wrist now, on a chain. His other hand held his gun pointed at the ground.

Sheriff McClellan was a clean-cut man, with a thick brow and a bold, Roman nose. He had proud features and tanned skin, hinting at more native heritage than his deputy kneeling by the two men Brenner had beaten.

McClellan frowned at her badge. "FBI?" he said slowly. And something in his tone shifted almost instantly. If she hadn't been paying attention, she might have missed it, or perhaps gotten whiplash.

Ella took it all in quickly. Suddenly, the Sheriff, still standing next to the prow of his green boat, seemed far more interested in her badge than the two men on the ground or even Brenner.

He was watching her from under his pronounced brow, his dark eyes narrowed. "Do you have a name?" he said.

Deciding to play on this sudden caution he was displaying, Ella didn't give her first name but said, "Agent Porter. And this is Marshal Gunn. He was attacked by these youths and defended himself."

McClellan glanced at the girl who'd called him *dad*. He raised an eyebrow as if questioning her. The girl looked disgusted and more than a little uneasy, but—to Ella's surprise—gave a quick nod, corroborating the claim.

The Sheriff slowly holstered his gun. The megaphone dropped with a *dunk* back into the boat, and he rubbed his hands off on his jeans.

"Well, well," he said, his tone congenial all of a sudden. "Boys will be boys, you know. They're younger than they look," he said, nodding to the two young men in the mud. "Good guys if you get to know them. Everyone's been a little bit antsy recently. I'm sure it's nothing, right?" he said conversationally, glancing at Brenner now. The same eyebrow trick.

Ella wasn't surprised to hear Brenner say, "I'm not looking to press charges if that's what you mean. They pulled steel—if *I* was in a bad mood, I woulda shot them."

"Asshole," muttered the one named Larry, rubbing at the side of his face.

The Sheriff stepped in front of him now, the same way Ella had done with Brenner.

Now, he stood a couple feet away from her, about at eye level due to the incline of the lake shore, his boots pressed in the mud. He was also concealing the knife on the ground.

Ella studied him. "How come people are antsy?" she said slowly.

"Hmm, what's that?"

"You said people have been antsy for a few days, how come?"

"Oh—nothing. Just local business. We've had a good few tourists recently. Normally we only get a few a month."

"Someone else came through recently?" Ella said innocently, remembering how the general store owner and the motel-keeper had both denied seeing Rose Lewis.

"Oh, you know—people come, people go. I think that young lady, there. Bronwyn, right? She's been here a couple of days. Larry's friend. Isn't that right, Lar?"

The man massaging his face just scowled at Brenner.

Ella said, "Did someone by the name of Rose Lewis come through here, recently?"

The Sheriff blinked. He scratched at his chin. "Can't say that I recognize that name."

Ella's expression remained polite. "But you knew hers, yes? You remember names?"

"Bronwyn? Oh, that's just because she was at the dance last night." He chuckled. "It's a small town—not much to do." He'd hitched his thumbs inside his belt now, creating impressions on his flannel. "Names get around," he added. "I didn't catch yours." He glanced past Ella now, studying where Mortimer Graves watched with his arms crossed.

Ella shot a quick look back and felt a cold chill all of a sudden. Graves was standing stiff as a poker, his hands clasped in front of him as if standing to attention in a parade line. But it was the look in his eyes that gave Ella pause.

Those same, dark hollows were now ever so faintly narrowed. If one hadn't already spent time with the Graveyard Killer, they might have missed it. But Mortimer wasn't blinking, wasn't even twitching. Like a hunting hound suddenly perked, pointing in the direction of wild game.

And he was facing the deputy crouched by the two men in the mud.

Chapter 9

"Where did you get that, if you don't mind me asking," Graves said slowly, his predatory eyes still locked on the deputy.

At first, Ella didn't know what the Graveyard Killer was referring to. But something in his tone sent more shivers up her spine. The sheriff seemed to have noticed something untoward in Graves' gaze now as well. "Excuse me? I didn't catch your name," McClellan said.

But Mortimer was still staring at his deputy. He took a sudden step forward, and another. One moment still and stiff like a poker, the next covering the distance from the stairs to Ella's side as if double-speed.

He spoke again, his tone carrying the same volume and cadence, but sounding colder and *louder* now that he was near Ella. "Where did you get that, young man?" he asked. "That bandanna."

Ella and Brenner shared a quick look. Her old friend's expression was equal part apologetic but confused. Ella, for her part, was struggling to keep track of the undercurrents in this conversation.

Like a placid lake, calm and unspoiled to the eye, but beneath the surface, *things* were happening which gave her chills, and she couldn't quite pinpoint the source of her discomfort.

Perhaps it was the Sheriff. The way he'd so quickly shifted his concerns when he'd spotted her badge. If anything, he wasn't even looking at Brenner anymore but staring at Ella, deciding she was the true threat.

FBI.

She'd seen the same reaction from drug lords or kingpins. The sorts of folk with a *lot* to lose when those three innocuous letters came along.

But a second undercurrent also swept by.

Mortimer was staring at a blue and red bandanna in the back of the deputy's belt. The item was hooked over the belt, looped twice and tied off. It wouldn't have been visible under his flannel shirt if he hadn't been helping the men in the mud.

Now, both the men that Brenner had floored had regained their breath and were rising on wobbly feet. They retreated a couple of steps, guided by the deputy towards where the sheriff's daughter had remained, watching but not participating.

Now, though, the deputy turned. The bald man noticed he was the one being addressed. His hand hovered over the bandanna briefly, and then he turned fully, adjusting his shirt to cover the bandanna and staring Mortimer Graves in the eyes. "And you are?" he said, frowning.

Graves didn't blink. "We'll get to that, I'm sure. Now answer my question; where did you get that cloth?"

The deputy scowled, wrinkling his nose. "I'm not sure I like your tone."

"Now, now," said the Sheriff. "The bandanna was a gift. From my wife. She makes them herself—you should see her sometime."

Graves was still staring at the deputy. He spoke now in a purr, like a lion in tall grass who's spotted two hunters that had wandered too close. "Is that true? You got the bandanna from his wife?"

The deputy blinked and scowled but shooting a look at his boss, he shrugged. "Yeah. Now, who the hell are you?"

Graves suddenly smiled.

It wasn't a pleasant expression. His lips peeled back slowly, like fresh earth pulled from tombstones. His perfectly white teeth flashed, and his eyes held a look of extreme amusement. "I see," he whispered slowly. "That's how it's going to be, then? You can call me Graves."

"You got a first name?" the deputy asked.

"That is my first name. And where do you live, hmm? Where can I find you later tonight?"

The deputy blinked at this comment. Ella hissed, turning sharply to stare at her unwanted companion. Graves just chuckled, holding up his hands now, his teeth still on display. "I tease. I tease. It's a pleasure to meet the two of you. Sheriff McClellan, is it? Tell your wife she's wonderful with her stitchwork."

"Yeah... yeah, I will. Now, say, you three must have just arrived, is that right?" The Sheriff didn't wait for anyone to respond. "I figure so. I'm sure we don't need to get into this little fracas here, huh? Just a couple of knuckleheads fighting over their ladies. Isn't that right, Larry?" The Sheriff said, laughing too loudly and patting Larry on the back with firm blows.

The young man winced but just nodded.

Ella considered this for a second. The Sheriff seemed intent on brushing this altercation under the rug. The way he'd charged to shore, gun in hand, she'd felt certain he'd want to drag Brenner away.

But the difference had been her badge.

FBI.

He knew as well as she did that they didn't have much in the way of backup out here. And even as she thought this, a chill trembled up her spine. Did she really think that she'd need backup as a Fed in a small American town?

She said, "I don't see any reason to cause trouble. Brenner?"

"Already said, I don't care about charges. I was playing nice."

Larry and his skinhead friend muttered darkly, but the deputy clapped both of them on their backs and they went quiet. The girl by the fishing boat was still shaking her head, muttering and rolling her eyes as if this whole business was beneath her.

"Well, you three were stopping by my office, right?" said the Sheriff conversationally. "I saw you up there. Just on a bit of a lunch break," he said, chuckling.

"You like catching your food fresh," said Graves, nodding. "I'm the same way."

"Huh. Yeah. Well..." The Sheriff shrugged. He stood awkwardly now. Everything in his posture screaming that he wanted them all to turn and leave.

Ella said, slowly, "We wanted to ask you about someone named Abraham. A young man—he had a bandage on his ear."

She nearly missed it, but the deputy tensed by the boat, frowning at the side of the Sheriff's face. But the Sheriff was a far more experienced poker player by the look of things. He just smiled. "Abraham... yeah... yeah, you must mean Helen's kid."

Brenner was nodding. "Yeah, Helen's kid. Abraham was at the dance last night, right?"

The Sheriff turned to him. "I... not sure where you're getting your information, Mr. Marshal. But I think so. I might've seen him there. No one named Rose, though," he added with a playful chuckle.

Brenner replied, "Where can we find Abraham?"

"Oh, you know—around. I think he works at the general store some days."

"We didn't see him there. Where's Helen? His mother, right?"

"Oh... hmm... yeah. She..." The Sheriff hesitated, glancing back at the deputy. The two of them both looked uncomfortable. Something passed between them though, and the deputy excused himself, slipping between Graves and Ella and hurrying back towards the office.

The Sheriff just watched him go, then, clearly stalling, said, "What was the question?"

"Where's he going?" Brenner asked, while at the same time Ella said, "Where's Helen's home?"

The Sheriff waved after his deputy. "Oh, just... gonna make a call. Unrelated case. We don't have much crime around here." He smiled brightly.

Ella glanced towards where she'd spotted the rusted knife in the mud. It was missing now. She looked back up, and repeated slowly so he couldn't dodge again, "Where's Helen's home?"

"Yeah... right, right. I can take you, if you like?"

"I don't feel as if that would be necessary—"

"Ah, no bother!" The Sheriff said brightly. "I'm on my lunch break anyhow. Here, let me change out of my boots and I can lead you to her. Helen loves guests."

"Is your deputy calling her and telling her we're coming?" Brenner said, blunt as ever.

Ella scowled at him but hid the expression when the Sheriff looked over. "Huh? What a lively imagination there, marshal. No, no. Another case. Here, you three just hang tight—let me grab my hiking shoes."

"Oh? Is it a bit of a walk?" Ella asked.

"Mhmm. Helen and her husband Don live near the hot springs, at the foot of Mount Sherman over there." He waved a hand generically away from the lake. "Should only be a brisk half-hour walk."

"Half hour?" Ella asked. "Do you have a car?"

"Not really. Couple of old mechanical rigs used for delivery jobs. That's about it." He flashed a smile that would have been charming in almost any other situation. "Things go at a different pace in Parcel. Just hang tight. Be right with ya."

He turned, taking the stairs two at a time, and slipped into the office, the glass door closing as he did. A figure stood in the door, a woman with big, puffy hair, wearing a red sweater, who watched it all nervously.

Ella recognized the desk clerk who'd greeted them initially before she'd spotted the commotion caused by Brenner.

Now, though, she stood between her two companions, feeling a slow weight settling in her stomach. The two young men behind her were getting into the boat with the Sheriff's daughter, still scowling at Brenner.

The Sheriff and his deputy had disappeared from sight in a right hurry, and now their attendant was watching through the glass, looking clearly uncomfortable.

In fact, as Ella glanced around, she spotted other faces watching them. People on the water, or walking around the lake, or sitting on their wooden front porches across the water.

All the eyes seemed to dart away when she looked, like minnows trained to swim for cover at the sight of a larger fish.

But that left one question... what type of large fish had trained the minnows?

Was there a shark in Parcel?

"Anyone getting a helluva creepy vibe from this place?" Brenner muttered beneath his breath, turning now to stare at the sheriff's office facing the lake.

"Perhaps bludgeoning the town youths isn't the *most* helpful deductive effort."

"Who the hell asked you, Graves?"

"Apologies, Mr. Gunn. I meant no offense."

"Yeah, well... Whatever. Who are you again? I don't know many CIs that fly helicopters."

"And I don't know many US marshals that partner with the FBI. Were you and Ella close growing up together in Nome?"

Ella interrupted sharply, frowning between the two men. "What was that business with the bandanna?" she asked.

"Hmm? Oh, that. Nothing, nothing."

"Graves... You promised. We're doing this my way. Remember? Arresting the culprit."

"As opposed to what?" Brenner said with a snort. "Letting 'God Save the Queen' over here go all repressed on their ass with a cricket bat?"

Graves smirked at this comment and shrugged. But he addressed Ella, hand over his heart, his perfectly manicured fingernails resting on his perfectly maintained suit. "What have I done to give any reason to doubt me, Eleanor?"

Ella just sighed, feeling the weight in her stomach intensifying. She felt in over her head... Far, far over her head.

But something was off in the town. She pressed her fingers against the note crinkling in her pocket. She thought of the footsteps, a young woman's, leading away from the only "motel" in the place. The creepy peeping Tom's lookout in the attic.

Something was definitely off.

The Sheriff was acting strange. His deputy too. The general store owner was strange. The motel-keeper was strange. The whole damn town was odd.

She shivered and shook her head. The note in her pocket had been signed *A*. And the young, handsome, blonde man with the injured ear had seemed embarrassed... maybe even guilty when he'd slipped away, but he'd lied for her—covered for Ella when she'd jumped out the window.

In this odd town, Abraham seemed like a potential ally. Or, at the very least, a source of information.

But up to this point, there'd been no sign of the claims that had brought them here.

Twenty girls missing?

The Sheriff was bragging about how *little* crime they had.

Something was very off, but Ella still didn't know what.

The door to the sheriff's office clattered open again. And now, wearing an official-looking brown jacket zipped halfway and matching hiking shoes, McClellan approached, gesturing for them to follow back up the path, away from the lake.

"This way, all! I'd offer the four-wheelers, but we've just got the two."

"ATVs?" Brenner asked.

"What's that?"

"Never mind."

Sharing uncomfortable looks with Brenner, Ella fell into step behind the sheriff. As she moved up the trail she shot a hesitant look back. Mortimer Graves was staring directly at the sheriff's office, motionless, watching through the glass with a look of extreme interest.

She felt another prickle along her skin. "Graves!" she snapped. "You coming?"

He looked at her, looked back to the sheriff's office, then said, "I think I might stay here a bit. See the sights. Speak to the locals."

Ella turned, hesitant. "Umm... You should come with us," she said *firmly.*

But then Graves looked up at her, smiled faintly, and turned on his heel, walking away from her around the lake, strolling casually with hands in his pockets. Every so often, though, he'd glance back to the sheriff's office where the deputy with the strange bandanna had disappeared.

"Shit," Ella said softly.

Brenner, at her side, muttered, "Want me to drag his ass along?"

She bit her lip. Part of her wanted to say yes. The last thing she needed was for Graves to be off on his own in town. What if this had all been some ruse just to get them here? To use her credentials as cover.

"Hey!" she called after him.

He didn't look back. He kept moving.

"Hey! I mean it!" She even took a few steps down the slope again, disheveling small stones and clumps of mud.

But Graves kept walking, waving over his shoulder. He turned briefly and made a motion over his chest.

Cross-my-heart.

Another promise. She thought back to the oath he'd given in the motel. Swearing on his eldest daughter. On everyone dear to him that he wouldn't break his word. That he wouldn't hurt a single hair on the head of whoever the culprit was—if there was one.

She had believed him then.

But it was like watching a shark slip beneath the waters in an in-ground swimming pool. A shark that had promised not to nip any of the children's toes splashing in the shallow end.

She opened her mouth to call out again, but he was now out of sight, having turned off the lake-side road and moving around the back of another lodge.

She shook her head in frustration.

"You all coming?" the Sheriff's voice called out from down the road.

"Dammit, dammit," Ella whispered to herself. And then she reached a decision. "Brenner, keep an eye on him, okay?"

"What, like leave you to follow him? Hell no."

"Please."

"No."

"Brenner, I'm begging you."

"Well, since you put it that way, *no, thank you.*"

Ella looked Brenner in the eyes. "I... I need you to watch him. He's... he's unstable."

"Who is he?"

"A CI, I told you."

"You're lying."

"I'm not!" she yelled in protest. She winced, dropping her voice. The two of them stood beneath the rustling leaves of a branch arching over them. She shifted uncomfortably, watching where the Sheriff had paused halfway down the path, pretending he wasn't trying to listen in.

"Please," she whispered more firmly. "I need someone to watch him. And someone needs to speak with Abraham."

"God dammit, Ella. Why do you keep doing shit like this? Just tell me the truth. Who is this guy? He's... off. Something is off about him. I knew guys with that look in their eyes in the frogmen."

"What sort of guys?"

"The ones who took potshots at women and children for the fun of it," Brenner said, cold. "I knew one guy that exclusively kept track of the women he shot. He once asked me if I thought their husbands were still crying. He seemed to like thinking about that shit."

Ella trembled now. "Well... then you should keep an eye on him, shouldn't you? If you think he's like *that*, then watch him."

"You don't seem concerned."

"Brenner, this is exactly what I look like when I'm concerned. I'm *completely* concerned. Now please, he's getting away."

"You need me."

"What?"

"God dammit, Ella. What happens if Sheriff Creepy over there goes all billy-club on you and I'm not around?"

Ella shook her head. "I've taken care of myself before. I'll do it again. I know how to fire this, you know." Her hand patted her gun.

Brenner looked down and up, shook his head and muttered, "This is stupid."

But then, he turned, and still shaking his head while muttering darkly, he moved off along the lake, hurrying in pursuit of Mortimer Graves.

Ella had just released a serial killer on the town because... because what? Of a hunch he was going to help them? Keep his word?

Or because...

He had saved her life twice?

She shook her head, caught between terror and frustration. She watched until Brenner slipped around behind the same lodge, disappearing in pursuit of the Graveyard Killer.

It wasn't until he was out of sight that Ella felt her stomach twist.

She hadn't told him to be careful, to watch out for Mortimer...

Then again, Brenner had the measure of the man. If anyone would be safe tailing the murderer, it was Gunn.

Using this to give her some amount of solace, alone now, she fell into step behind the sheriff, who smiled brightly and continued guiding her up the trail, away from the lake towards the hot springs and towards the home of Abraham's mother.

Chapter 10

Ella checked her phone as she trudged up the path outside the small, log-beam house. No signal. She raised the phone a bit, then felt silly. Of course there was no signal. They were in the middle of nowhere.

She lowered her hand, pocketing the phone, then glancing ahead towards where the sheriff had paused by a small, wooden gate. The wooden fence served as an armrest where he leaned, and he toed the gate open, gesturing for her to enter.

"Not sure Helen's home," he said conversationally.

Ella paused, glancing down the branching path. Ahead, she spotted steam rising over trees. "Are those the hot springs?" she asked.

"Hmm? Oh—yes, yes. Private, though. Some renovations."

She frowned. "Renovations to the springs?"

"To the greeting center." He waved a hand dismissively and then used it to gesture through the open gate. "After you," he said conversationally.

She hesitated, glancing back along the trail, breathing slowly. It had only taken them about twenty minutes to reach the house. Partially, because the sheriff had taken a left turn at a fork and Ella had realized it would only loop around the same path a second time.

She'd asked about it, and, laughing uneasily, he'd said the warmth was getting to him. A long day. And then he'd gone right. They'd arrived ten minutes faster than he'd said they might.

She stepped through the gate, shooting a quick look back at McClellan, studying his olive-skinned features and bold, Roman nose. "Who did you have to call?" she said conversationally.

"What? Back at the office? Just a small case."

"What case?"

He frowned but quickly hid the expression. "Mostly inside baseball."

She nodded once. "I see." She then turned her back to the gate and to the Sheriff, peering towards the small plot of land upon which the log-beam home was set. A welcome mat sat squarely in front of a wooden door. A stone well sat off to the side, near a vegetable garden with ground cover, tomatoes and what looked like beans. She spotted some dust along the side of the well, looking at this curiously, then approached the front door to the log home.

Her knuckles tapped against the frame. "Hello!" she called out. "FBI!"

She stepped back, waiting.

No sound. No response.

The Sheriff was standing by the gate still, leaning on the hand-built wooden fence while picking at his fingernails. Again, he had the look of a man pretending to be disinterested but watching her every movement out of his peripheral vision.

She muttered under her breath, "Sheriff Creepy..." repeating the moniker Brenner had ascribed. But now, considering Brenner, she felt a jolt of guilt. She never should have come here... she knew that. But it had seemed like the only call. It wasn't like she had much backup with Chief Baker.

Baker was married to Priscilla, her sister. And she still wasn't sure *who* had hired the hitman to attack her.

But she couldn't go to her superiors either. She'd been banished to Nome exactly *because* she'd let the Graveyard Killer go. If they'd known she'd done it on purpose, they would have arrested her on the spot.

The guilt weighed heavily. But now... it was as if someone had given her a shovel just to watch her dig her own grave.

She knocked louder this time, fist thumping against the door. "Hello! FBI!"

Still no response. She turned to glance towards the fence. The Sheriff just shrugged sheepishly at her, calling out. "Sorry! Guess she isn't home."

"I bet she isn't," Ella muttered beneath her breath. But she smiled back, waving. And turned to face one of the windows, stepping to the left. The drapes were closed. Lace, intricately knitted and beautifully silky white. But she couldn't see past them. She frowned, moving around the side of the house now.

She heard the gate *creak* suddenly and the sound of hastening footsteps, suggesting the Sheriff was following. Nervous, too, by the sound of it.

"Good," she muttered.

She was here not because of the Graveyard Killer. Not to protect her career, she reminded herself. For the same reason she'd let him go to begin with. Not only had he saved her life, but he'd also saved many *other* lives. The people who, more often than not, Ella was only introduced to in a morgue.

She didn't know if what she was doing was right.

She doubted it.

But sometimes, in a cold world, it felt like there were no other options except the ones conjured in a person's mind.

She found a smaller window, set lower and peered through. This one had been blocked by books. She frowned now, rapping her knuckles against the glass. "Hello!" she said louder. "Anyone home?"

The sheriff appeared in *front* of her. Suggesting instead of following her, he'd circled around the house the other way, cutting off any further progress. He was breathing a bit heavily, meaning he'd probably jogged.

Through quick breaths, trying to appear as nonchalant as possible, he said, "Like I said earlier, Helen might be out. Abraham too."

Ella glanced at the sheriff, back at the house. "So Abraham lives here with his mother?"

"I... oh... Umm... I don't know."

"You said Abraham would be out, too. Meaning he probably lives here too, right?"

"I couldn't say, really."

Ella frowned at him. He smiled back. For a moment, she felt how Brenner must have whenever she confronted his glare with a pleasant veneer. She wasn't sure she liked the experience.

Her hand moved slowly to her holster now, tracing the seams, tapping against the comforting weight. Alone out here, with no communications, her unease was rising. Exhaustion, too. Not much more than twenty-four hours ago, she'd found herself marching into a blizzard.

Briefly, she thought of her cousin, Madison Porter. The girl had lost a toe to frostbite but had taken it in good stride.

Ella's twin sister had been the one to spearhead the attempt to rescue Maddie off the side of that mountain. Ella had been so caught up with catching a killer, looking back, she felt as if she'd neglected her higher duty of rescuing her cousin.

Was this absolution? Breaking every law of common sense to come out here on a strange helicopter with only one friendly face to have her back?

There was no sign of Rose Lewis.

Ella considered her options, glancing again towards the blockaded window of the small house. She then gestured at it. "Think you can gain us entry? I want to look around."

The sheriff blinked. "I... I'm afraid without probable cause..."

"It's a wellness check," Ella shot back. "Abraham's face was injured when I saw him last. I want to make sure he's okay."

"Abraham doesn't live here."

"You made it sound like he did."

"He doesn't."

The Sheriff's smile was gone, and he was watching her now with cold eyes. She returned the look, feeling a slow tremor along her fingers near her holster.

Did she want to push the issue? Something about the log house, door locked, windows blocked, seemed to whisper shenanigans.

But the Sheriff had come along to keep an eye on her. Maybe if they came back later tonight?

And then suddenly, the sound of an opening door. A voice. "Hello? Who's back there? Sheriff McClellan, is that you?"

Ella turned sharply and found herself staring at a portly woman with a pleasant face and a white bonnet. The woman had on a large, white apron, pristine as the silk in the window, and was smiling. "Hello there, dearie. I don't think I've had the pleasure. I'm Helen Kay."

Ella took a step back if only to keep an eye on the two figures. The Sheriff around the right side of the house, and now Helen Kay around the left.

"Didn't you hear us?" Ella asked carefully.

"Hmm? Hear? Oh my, were you knocking on the door? I'm so sorry—I'm a very heavy sleeper."

Ella gestured towards the woman's apron. "Looks like you were in the kitchen."

The woman just smiled. "Oh, no—sorry. A bit of a stain on my shirt. Just didn't want to speak with guests looking slovenly. I heard you say you wanted to speak with Abraham?" The round face suddenly frowned in disapproval. "He hasn't done anything naughty has he?"

Ella paused briefly. "Where is your son?"

"Oh, somewhere I'm sure. He likes wandering the mountains."

"He looked injured. What happened to his ear?"

"A shaving accident. My, my, missie. You sure do have a lot of questions." The woman chuckled but didn't look offended.

Which she *should* have, Ella decided. Unless she *knew* Ella was FBI. But another civilian, prying bluntly, directly? It would have offended anyone.

Had the deputy called ahead? She wondered if the town had its own landlines. Or perhaps walkie-talkies.

She said, "Mind if I look in the house?"

"Certainly," Helen said. "You're more than welcome to look around. Abraham isn't home."

Ella bit her lip, and she thought she caught the faintest of glances shared between the Sheriff and the woman, but distractedly, Ella moved around the side of the house, taking the stairs and peering through the open door.

Chapter 11

Helen bustled hurriedly up after her, prattling, "Sorry if it's a bit of a mess. Been doing cleaning today while the boys are out."

"Boys?" Ella questioned, reminded again of the sheriff's earlier insistence that Abraham did not live with his mother, Helen.

"Oh, yes. My son, Abraham, and my husband."

"Who's your husband?"

"I'm sure you haven't met him, dearie. Here—here, careful for the spill."

Ella stared at the ground. Soap and slick water spread across the floor. A mop in one corner. A bucket next to it. Towels everywhere.

She hesitated, glancing around the small, cramped space. "Cleaning, huh?" she said slowly.

In one corner of the room, she spotted a wooden table.

Helen gestured at it. "Oh, yes—venison. Butchered a five-point buck last night. Had to clean to make sure we don't get that gamey smell. Not like last time, huh, Brandon?"

"No, Helen," said the sheriff's voice, and Ella started, turning sharply to realize McClellan was right behind her. Far closer than made her comfortable.

She stepped away from the door, frowning at the slick ground, and the table where apparently a buck had been butchered.

It was all off, but now, Ella wasn't sure if she'd find anything in the house... Why was Helen inviting her in?

Unless this was a bluff. A last-ditch attempt to keep her away...

This small, portly woman, though?

Ella wrinkled her nose. She looked more like someone's doting mother than a killer...

Yet... twenty young women missing according to Mortimer. If his information could be trusted. She still didn't know the source.

But then, Ella bit her lip and moved, stepping into the house. Her blood pumping. She didn't wait for invitation either. She walked across the slick floor, apologizing briefly but then marching towards the side of the house which had been blockaded by the books in the window.

"Oh—hang on a moment!" said Helen excitedly.

But Ella just shot a look back and said, "Don't mind me. Just taking you up on that invite to look around."

She reached a door, tried the door knob. Locked. She frowned and gestured at it. "What's this room?"

"That? Oh—that's Abraham's. He sometimes locks it when he leaves."

Ella shook her head. "I need it open."

"I'm afraid he has the only key."

"Mhmm. I'll go through the window then. That work for you?"

"I... oh... umm... Oh, look—silly me. He left his key right here, see?"

Ella frowned as the woman pretended to pick something off the mantelpiece, but she'd obviously had it in her palm. A small brass key appeared and was handed to Ella. Ella took the key, forcing a smile of her own, hoping it was a disarming expression, then slipped the key into the lock, turning it.

Click.

The door creaked on old hinges as she pushed it with her shoulder. She kept an eye on Helen to her right and on the Sheriff who was still lingering in the doorway.

And then she stepped into Abraham's bedroom.

A spartan affair.

A hand-hewn bed frame in the corner, with a simple mattress. The blankets were neatly folded and a pillow rested perfectly symmetrically with the headboard. A closet to the side, displaying neat sets of shirts and two pairs of boots beneath them, both also perfectly arranged. The window itself was covered with books she'd seen from the outside. Ella frowned at these.

Books on history, mostly. Famous battles, the Civil War, the War of 1812.

She approached a dresser and opened the top drawer. Socks, each paired, neatly laid out. The next drawer was shirts. Then pants.

She frowned, glancing around the room, then turned back to look at Helen. "You have a very neat son," Ella said slowly.

"Thank you, thanks. We try, of course. The sun guides us."

Ella hesitated. "The sun?" She paused but received no response. Not that she needed it—her mind was moving rapidly. The Dawkins cult which had gone missing in that plane all those years ago had broadcast more than one message about the guidance of the sun. Following the sun.

Ella paused, shifting. "Do you know someone named Rose Lewis?"

"Who?"

"So that's a no?"

"I guess not. I know everyone in town."

"But tourists come through."

"Occasionally, yes. I hear about them mostly. All the way out here, we only really head into town when we're needed. I'm a cleaner." She smiled, leaning against the door frame.

Ella nodded slowly, her eyes moving up to the woman's fingers. A faint rusty ring around the nails. Flecks of red.

Fingerpaint?

Or blood?

Helen noticed Ella's gaze and waved her hand. "Oh, you know—I help with skinning the doe. There's an old expression. I think I heard it's from Mr. Lincoln himself."

"Abraham Lincoln?"

"Yes—if you can't skin the deer, hold a leg." Helen chuckled, but her hands moved and tucked in her apron. "So what is it you wanted with Abraham again?"

Ella bit her lip, glancing around a final time. She spotted what looked like a loose floorboard, but when she stepped on it, she realized it was simply a warp in the wooden plank.

"We harvest the trees ourselves," said Helen conversationally.

"Pretty big trees, some of them. I've seen 'em."

"Oh, the ones near the main lake are *nothing* compared to the giants at the sacred spring up on—"

"Excuse me!" The sheriff called suddenly from the door. "Agent Porter, right? We should probably let Helen get back to her work, hmm?"

Ella shot a quick look past Helen through the open doors of the two other rooms visible in the hall. One to a master bedroom, also clean. Also empty. One to a private bathroom. Both doors thrown open as if boasting they had nothing to hide.

So why did it feel like this whole damn town was concealing something?

Ella gave a final look into the bedroom. Glancing at the books. As she did, she spotted something. A small fragment of parchment—yellowed. Barely visible if she hadn't been looking for it and aware of its type due to the note she already had in her pocket.

Used as a bookmark for the historical tome on the Civil War, the piece of yellow paper barely jutted past the seam.

Ella stared at it, then approached slowly, pretending as if she were looking out the window. "It's a beautiful view of the hot springs," Ella said over her shoulder.

"Thank you, of course! I wish you could see them. But they're closed for a private ceremony."

"I thought it was closed for renovations," Ella murmured, cautiously peeling the note from inside the book, wincing as it crinkled.

"What? Oh—umm... yes. Mhmm."

"Agent Porter!" the sheriff called again.

"Coming!" she replied.

Ella pocketed the note, pressing it against her leg, and then turned, flashing a quick smile at the matriarch before sidestepping and joining the sheriff in the hall.

The man had braved the suds and thin veneer of water in the main room, standing at the entrance to the corridor now while frowning at her, breathing slowly. He cast a glance over his shoulder, scratching at the back of his head, then gestured with one hand towards the door. "After you," he murmured.

She repeated the smile, the nod, and then moved across the water, keeping track of the figures behind her by using the reflections in the windows. Another quick glance was exchanged between the two figures, and Ella exited the wooden home with no small amount of relief.

The sheriff was lingering back, talking in muted tones to Helen, and Ella used this as her chance to slip around the side of the wooden structure and pull the note from her pocket. Her back to the door to shield it from view, she unfurled the yellow paper.

In the same quick handwriting she'd seen on the first letter, she read, simply:

They chose you. Rose, you need to go! Get out of

And the letter stopped mid-sentence. Ella frowned, turning the parchment over, but there was nothing else written. She re-read the strange words, staring at the note. Who'd sent this?

She shook her head slowly, sighing with a puff of air. Abraham. The answer was clear.

The last letter had been marked A. Abraham had been there, outside the motel. And now in Abraham's bedroom, this note, hidden in a book. An unfinished letter, though... as if...

Ella tilted her eyes to look up at the clouds floating across the blue horizon. The afternoon sunlight warmed her cheeks. The civil war book beneath the window had hardly been a great hiding spot. The sentence half cut off...

Abraham must have been interrupted while writing it.

So why hadn't he finished it?

Unless he'd known it was too late. He had known Rose, to whom the letter was addressed, was beyond warning. Because he'd known something had happened to her.

"What's that you got there?"

She turned sharply, palming the note and slipping it into her pocket in a smooth motion. The sheriff had moved quietly, far quieter than she would've thought possible on the wet ground.

He was now stepping off the bottom stair, leaving dark footprints where the moisture seeped into the oak.

"Oh, nothing," Ella said quietly. "I still need to speak to Abraham."

"Well, it might be late by the time he gets back. And then, he'll probably head to the dance in town."

Ella watched the sheriff.

He smoothed his thick beard, his dark eyes fixated on her, unblinking.

She kept her expression congenial, but said, "The dance tonight, got it." She shifted from one foot to the other, then said, frowning. "Just a quick question, Sheriff."

"Mhmm?"

"Do you know anything about the Dawkins cult?" as she asked, she watched his expression closely.

The sudden change in topic, the out-of-the-blue query, had its intended effect. Briefly taken aback, he blinked as if startled. His eyes darted towards the well on the premises, then flicked off over the fence in the direction of the hot springs.

But to her surprise, it wasn't an expression of guilt.

Rather, it was one of fear. He licked his lips slowly, staring at her, breathing heavily. And then he tried to cover, but it was too late, and they both knew it.

"The what?" he said slowly, but the color had gone from his face.

Ella watched him, her eyes darting up the porch towards where Helen was frowning in the doorway, a mop clutched tightly in one pudgy palm. Standing there in her apron and bonnet, clutching the mop, she looked something like a queen with a scepter—it was in her eyes.

Sheriff McClellan gazed at Ella, staring, but volunteering nothing else until he'd swallowed once, stared directly at her and insisted. "Never heard of them. Is that a band?"

Ella didn't look away. She knew he was lying, and he knew that she knew.

And in that moment, as Sheriff McClellan watched her, she felt a shiver crawl up her spine. A slow sense of discomfort settled on her, heavy, like a rain coat. She'd overplayed her hand. She was alone, without backup.

The sheriff said, cautiously, "Who have you been talking to?"

"About what? You don't know the Dawkins cult, right?"

But the look in his eyes returned. Not guilt, not as if he was hiding something. But a supreme look of fear.

Then, suddenly, he moved fast. His hand darted towards his holster, reaching for his weapon. Ella, startled, didn't bother going for hers.

They were close enough that she surged forward, moving purely on instinct.

Her foot lashed out.

McClellan was in the middle of shouting, "You're under arres—oomph!"

The air left his lungs and he doubled over in pain as her foot caught him between the legs. Only then did Ella draw her own weapon, pointing it at McClellan and raising her own voice, "Hands up, *now.*" She couldn't help but add, as if compulsively impelled to, "*please.*"

Her gun wavered, moving towards the porch, then back again at the groaning sheriff. Helen didn't budge but, rather, watched with a look of some disdain.

Ella breathed slowly, her heart pounding, feeling a slow prickle of warmth along her cheeks. She shot a glance over her shoulder to the garden path, her gaze tracing past that stone well, off in the direction of the hot springs.

She stood motionless for a moment and then reached a decision. She darted in, grabbed the sheriff's weapon from his holster, tutting when he tried to resist. Then, slipping her stolen gun into her belt, she backed away, moving quickly, but keeping her eyes on the two townies.

"You're making a mistake!" the sheriff called after her.

But Ella kept going. She breathed slowly, uncertain what to do. Mc-Clellan, in a way, was in his right to attempt to keep the peace in his town. He hadn't technically done anything illegal...

But something was off. Something in this town was terribly, terribly wrong. She glanced in the direction of the hot springs. Renovations? Rituals? The stories she was receiving weren't lining up.

Keeping her gun trained towards McClellan, she only broke into a jog when she was sure he wasn't reaching for a secondary.

Then, gun holstered, she broke into a run.

Not back to town. But towards the hot springs.

As she ran, a voice yelled after her, bleeding with conviction, "You're making a mistake!"

Chapter 12

Brenner kept his distance, sticking to the shadows of the trees, eyes on his moving target. Just like the old days—though back then, there had been far fewer trees and far more hills, scrubby vegetation and often sand.

Up here, in Parcel, things weren't nearly as hot as they'd been while on tour overseas. Ahead, he spotted the man named Graves strolling along in the woods. They'd doubled back around the lake, twice. Graves had paused a few times to peer through the windows of some of the homes. But for the most part, he had been stalling.

And now, Brenner knew what for.

They were following the deputy with the bandanna tied to his belt.

Mortimer Graves kept at a safe distance, moving through the trees, off the trail, following the deputy ever since he'd left the small sheriff's office. He now hastened up a path leading away from the wide lake.

Brenner watched, impressed, as Graves used shadows, motion and line of sight to perfectly conceal himself whenever the deputy shot a glance over his shoulder, nervous and fidgety.

Brenner watched from a distance as well and felt a growing sense of unease.

Ella's CI was a bit *too* good at following the deputy. Like a panther stalking through tall grass or a hunter with his scope targeting an unsuspecting doe. This well-dressed Brit was someone who'd done this before, and it made Brenner uneasy.

The only sorts he'd known overseas with the care, the caution, of a tracker with the confidence and charisma of a luxury car salesman had been with the CIA.

But Mr. Graves wasn't government. That much bled through the man's very pores—no... this was a different creature altogether.

The deputy moved up a trail, walking hurriedly now. Brenner kept off the road, moving through the forest, under giant boughs and thick branches and over root humps rising from the mud and grass. Mortimer did much the same, about two hundred yards ahead, none the wiser to his pursuer.

To their right, Brenner spotted a small log home with a stone well out front. The door to the home was closed. Ahead, he spotted signs of the hot springs—wafting steam on the air.

The deputy was marching towards the hot springs. Now, the bald man with the pinched face was no longer glancing over his shoulder but was practically power-walking up the trail, past the small log house and towards the hot springs. The distant mountains looked blue against the horizon, the peaks touching clouds moving lazily under the sun.

Brenner kept moving silently but was briefly distracted by the log home with the stone well. Someone was watching them through the window. A round face wearing a bonnet. The moment the figure spotted Brenner's attention, she ducked out of sight.

He felt a faint shiver along his back and shook his head. People in this town gave him the creeps.

"Why are you following me?"

Brenner stumbled, pulling up sharp and hissing under his breath. Distracted by the woman in the log cabin, he'd lost focus.

And now the expensive-suit-wearing gentleman with the dead eyes was staring straight at him, having emerged from behind a thick oak.

Brenner had gone still as well, his feet pressed into detritus. Leaves fluttering across his work boots. The difference between the men's shoes struck Brenner as laughable. Multi-thousand dollar loafers with some Italian brand name Brenner likely couldn't pronounce, compared to his own, decade-old, well-worn, mud-stained work boots.

Brenner was a few inches taller than Mortimer, but Graves was standing on higher ground, on the incline, and so they stood eye to eye.

Another tree fringe behind Brenner, which he'd passed as Graves had spoken, now concealed the two of them from the log cabin's line of sight.

In a way, this provided privacy... it also meant there would be no witnesses.

But Brenner wasn't the scaring sort. He shrugged once. He wasn't the deceptive sort, either. Blunt, some said. Honest, he thought.

"Ella told me to," he replied.

Mortimer's hands were folded over each other. He watched Brenner with those cold, dark eyes of his. "I don't need a babysitter," Mortimer replied slowly, still speaking in that clipped accent.

Brenner shrugged. "Not my call."

"Well... now it is, perhaps—no? I don't see Eleanor."

"Where do you know her from?" Brenner said, deciding he might as well go on the offensive. His heart was still pounding from being startled. He didn't like the *feeling* of fear.

"Eleanor? We go back. So do you."

"She didn't want us talking about that."

"I'm not asking." Graves shook his head, his neatly trimmed hair barely shifting, suggesting he used some sort of product. "I can tell."

"Right. Same way you can tell about people's feelings, huh?"

Graves flashed a smile. A crocodile smile—all teeth, no eyes. "Quite. Well, Mr. Gunn, you and I seem to have reached an impasse. You seem intent on following me, but I'm intent on *not* being followed."

Brenner nodded. "That's a real pickle, isn't it." He remained standing exactly where he was, boots at shoulder width, pressed into the leaves and small branches. The dirt trail off to his left continued to meander off in the direction of the mountains and the hot springs, but Brenner ignored it.

Then, deciding he wanted to continue the offensive, Brenner said, "What's with the bandanna?"

"Excuse me?"

"You recognized it. That's what got you all itching about the deputy. What's the bandanna?"

Mortimer studied Brenner. "I see. So she doesn't just keep you around as a trained ape. That's nice to know."

Brenner snorted. "Me think good."

Mortimer Graves smiled this time, and for a moment, it actually looked genuine. He shrugged once, his suit sleeves only faintly crinkling with the motion. "The bandanna belonged to an acquaintance of mine."

"A friend?"

"I don't have those. Not really."

"Okay. What sort of acquaintance, and how do you know it was his?"

"A private investigator," Graves said slowly. "Now, see, I've been forthright with you. How about you extend me an olive branch of trust, and I'll be on my way without having to resort to anything beneath the both of us..."

Brenner tensed, his hand hovering near his holster. "That sounded like a threat."

"Not at all," Graves replied. "I don't strike first, Mr. Gunn. And from what I can tell about you, I suspect you're far faster with that weapon of yours than I'd like to think."

This time, Brenner flashed the crocodile grin, leaning against the tree now, one leg crossing over the other in a posture of extreme ease. "Good guess," he said with a smirk.

"You won't let me leave, I take it?"

"I mean... do what you want, man. I just might stroll along. What are you going to do with that deputy?"

"Nothing. Ask."

"Which is it? Nothing or ask?"

Mortimer's eyes flashed. He seemed to be losing his patience now, and his lips formed a thin line. The man wasn't quite handsome, but he wasn't ugly either. He had pleasant but unremarkable features. But there was something in those eyes that unsettled Brenner in a way that few things could. "What type of bastard are you?" Brenner said slowly.

"Pardon me?"

"You're a bastard. I mean that politely, of course. But a damn bastard. And I'm trying to figure out what type. Are you the type I gotta look out for coming from behind or the front?"

Graves studied Brenner a second, and then said, slowly, "Have you heard the adage *just choose the time and place*?"

"Yeah. Why? You want to fight? We're a bit sober for that."

"Certainly. What I mean is, the type of... man I am is the sort that would choose the time and place." Graves stepped slowly onto the road now, scraping a foot through the dust and staring curiously at the arching pattern of disheveled earth.

"And what time and place is that?"

"Generally, when someone is asleep would be my preferred time. And the place? Where I'm least expected." He didn't smile now but just spoke slowly, as if trying to communicate something important. "So no, Mr. Gunn. I have no intention of fighting you."

Brenner was still leaning against the tree, feeling the rough pattern of the bark against his shoulder. He watched the strange man from hooded eyes, having gone still now, listening intently. "Sounds like another threat."

"That time... I suppose it was. Now, Mr. Gunn, I'm going to leave. And I'm going to request you don't follow me." He held up a hand primly and said, "Before you say, *or what,* let me preemptively explain how—"

He never managed to finish what had started as a promising sentence.

Instead, in the distance, the two of them heard the sound of a loud *crack,* and then a yell of pain.

Brenner broke into a sprint, shoving past Mortimer Graves. He recognized that voice.

"Ella!" he yelled, sprinting forward, kicking up dust.

The sound vanished though. And all that remained on the wind was the ominous silence and the reverberating echo of the painful shout.

Chapter 13

Ella clutched at her arm, wincing and gasping and cursing a million different ways. Small twigs tumbled around her, leaves twirling down from where she'd fallen. No sign of the sheriff—he hadn't passed by when she'd hidden in the branches.

But another figure had hurried past only moments before. In between curses, she frowned off down the trail, towards the switchback where the bald man with the pinched face—the deputy—had hurried past only moments before.

In fact, it was her curiosity that had caused her tumble, enticing her to lean too far forward, hand braced against a branch. The thing had snapped, but for the moment, the deputy didn't appear down the road to discover the source of the commotion. *Other* sounds continued to murmur behind her. The same, ominous sounds that had caused her to clamber up the tree in the first place.

The sheriff was nowhere in sight. His deputy had passed by only moments before. And the faint hush murmur of chanting continued to echo through the grove coming from the direction of the hot springs.

Still, Ella hissed in pain, glaring at the scrapes along her hands and lifted the edge of her shirt to frown at where her pale skin had been lashed with red. Even so, she held her tongue, trying to bite back another cry.

The ten foot fall from where she'd hidden herself in the lower boughs of the tree had elicited an unwanted cry. But now, the slow chanting murmur she'd heard from the direction of the hot springs seemed almost to grow louder, temporarily drowning her out.

Ella held her breath, listening, peering past the large tree she'd scaled, but unable to spot much in the way of movement. The thick grove's branch arms extended to block her view. The slow sound of chanting continued to waft on the wind, though. And occasionally, her cheeks speckled with moisture—droplets of warmth ushered by zephyrs.

She exhaled slowly, wincing again and rubbing at her arm.

Thumping footsteps alerted her to a new arrival, and she spun around, scraped and throbbing hand darting to her holster. Her fingers went still when she spotted a familiar, handsome face, cold blue eyes widened in something of a panic—a very unfamiliar expression on Brenner Gunn's normally stoic features.

But as he drew nearer, kicking up leaves, he slowed, glancing through the trees then back at her.

"Are you alright?" he called out.

But she held a finger to her lips, giving a quick nod, but jerking a thumb over her shoulder.

Brenner slowed, frowning, but kept stalking towards her, moving quietly on the dusty path, avoiding leaves and fallen branches. He also glanced at the trail, evidently noting the bootprints leading up the road where the deputy had disappeared. His frown turned to a look of concern as his eyes landed on her.

"Are you okay—I heard you shout," he said as he drew within a few feet and stopped.

Ella nodded a single time. "I fell."

"From the tree?"

"Yeah."

"Why were you in a—"

"Shh, keep it down. They might hear us."

"They? Wait... I hear it. What is that? Is that a choir?"

Ella shrugged, shaking her head and brushing her blond bangs aside. "I don't know," she whispered softly. "But it's been going on for a few minutes."

Brenner wrinkled his nose, cautiously stepping off the path and joining Ella in the soft padding of tumbled leaves.

Ella didn't want to mention she'd scaled a tree out of fright. Out of fear that Sheriff McClellan might be pursuing her. In a way, taking a higher lookout felt like a very Brenner thing to do.

But now, hands stinging, side throbbing, hair disheveled she just felt silly.

The chanting from the hot springs was quieting now but continued. Another voice was speaking, but Ella couldn't quite make out the sound. She began moving through the trees, cautiously, keeping crouched as she did, and gesturing for Brenner to follow.

He did, but as he fell into step, she shot a quick look back. "Where's Graves?"

Brenner hesitated, also turning. "Shit. He gave me the slip."

"You lost him?" she paused, one hand braced against a low divide in a gnarled oak.

"Yeah. Dammit. He was right there."

"You lost *him*?" she repeated, but this time the words carried far more inflection. Her own panic was rising to match the look Brenner's gaze had displayed earlier. Her mind filled with horrible thoughts. She'd needed Brenner to keep an eye on the serial killer.

Now... a murderer was loose in a small town with an even smaller law enforcement office.

"He was following the deputy," Brenner whispered, leaning against the same tree, but occasionally shooting uncomfortable looks back down the trail as if searching out something. He shook his head with a sigh. "We heard you scream—came running."

"I did *not* scream."

"You did."

"No—I fell and yelled in pain."

"So you *are* hurt?" he looked at her, concern in his eyes again.

"I'm fine."

The concern was quickly replaced by the same curiosity they both clearly felt, which dragged them closer towards the strange chanting coming from the off-limits hot springs. McClellan had said the springs were closed for renovations to an outbuilding. Helen had said some ritual was taking place.

They had both seemed secretive about it.

About everything.

Abraham still was fresh on Ella's mind, and she felt the parchment crinkling against her hip as she continued forward. Mortimer going missing only compounded her worries. The fact that her phone had no reception only increased her sense of isolation out in this strange and odd place.

Finally, the sheriff's reaction to the Dawkins cult had chilled her blood. Not guilt, as if he were somehow a secret participant. But fear. He knew the name, and he dreaded it.

How did it all come together? What was she missing?

That same curiosity prompted them to the tree line, emerging in a sparser section of the grove. The two of them remained a few trees deep, standing in the shadows. Brenner reached out, gently nudging her to the side, likely to give her a better hiding spot. As a trained sniper who'd worked with a spotter for five years, Brenner knew a thing or two about locating lookout spots.

As his hand grazed her elbow, Ella glanced down. For a moment, his fingers lingered longer than they might have done otherwise. She didn't pull away.

But then, the warmth of his hand, the comforting touch became secondary.

"What the hell..." she murmured.

Brenner cleared his throat, apologizing quickly, looking flustered, but she shook her head, pointing, and he realized the source of her surprise.

Twenty figures, all of them in red robes, stood around geysers in the ground. The hot springs poured down marble shelves, the water spilling together in milky, warm pools which shed trails of steam skyward. Three of these expansive marble shelves stretched out as wide as football fields. Each rising like a plateau, moving higher towards the mountains. The underground water sprang from small, dark caverns pockmarking the base of one of the largest, blue mountains.

The pristine, white marble foundations, serving as the weathered chutes which carried the water through the multi-level pools, glistened and sparkled where caught by the afternoon sunlight, as if starlight had been trapped in the smooth, white stone.

Geysers lined the springs, occasionally protruding from portions of the white marble, between rivulets and streams, blowing bursts of steam towards the sky on occasion. Ella wasn't quite sure if there was some underground magma flow near the surface, if the residents of the town stoked the springs themselves unnaturally, or if some other geological feature allowed the heat to perpetually warm the milky, blue water—the opaqueness created by what she assumed were mineral deposits carried down the mountain.

The many small waterfalls, the acres of pristine, glistening white stone, like gigantic, carved pearls, was breathtaking to behold.

But the twenty figures lining the lowest pool, facing the largest waterfall, and staring into the mineral-dense water behind a cloud of steam were the most eye-catching of it all.

Their faces were hidden by red masks matching the outfits. Their hands, hidden by gloves. Each of the figures carried a golden walking stick which they tapped occasionally against the ground. One figure stood apart from the rest, his feet in the water, his hands raised to the sky.

He was chanting something, and along with him, the others joined in.

As Ella stared at this strange spectacle, the man's voice exclaimed, "From the earth!"

The others all echoed back, "From the sun!"

The leader, standing ankle deep in the water continued, "From the heart!"

And the rest of them replied, "From the womb!"

The same sequence of exchange echoed again. And again. They kept repeating this back-and-forth chant, first the leader, then the rest. Occasionally, though Ella couldn't determine why, the walking sticks would tap against the white stone, the gilded handles flashing.

Brenner was breathing quietly at her side, his shoulder pressed to hers. The two of them were making use of a Y in a tree, their faces peering through this gap, fixated on the strange gathering.

Suddenly, there was a shout.

"Excuse me! No—hang on! Stop! You'll want to hear this!"

Ella's eyes darted to a familiar figure, shouldering his way through the ranks of red-robed chanters. The crowd didn't part, but masked faces turned, staring. Slowly, a hush fell over the gathering, and looks of accusation fixated on the newcomer.

"The deputy," Brenner whispered.

Ella nodded. The deputy was wiping at his face with a bandanna, before placing it back in his belt. He was breathing heavily, his pants stained with dirt. He looked very much out of place in his casual, fisherman's outfit, facing these red-robed, chanting figures.

Soon, as silence fell completely, the figure standing in the water looked down at the man. The figure in the water didn't speak, and when he had, Ella hadn't recognized his voice.

The deputy looked up, a few feet lower due to the way the pool and shelf of pristine marble worked.

Stuttering, the deputy said, "You guys are gonna want to head back to the mountain lake."

Everyone stared at him. Now, the only sound was that of the deputy's heavy breathing and the faint babble of water tumbling into the pools, along the chutes of marble, and spreading out from the blue mountain like a wedding gown's trail.

The deputy stammered. "I-I know we're not supposed to interrupt. But... the sheriff wanted me to tell you. You guys need to head back up. Okay? I know we have a deal, and all that. But there's Feds in town."

This time, his words seemed to get a reaction. The deputy nodded firmly, wagging his head up and down. "Yeah—yeah, exactly! Feds. Federal officers. Cops. You guys are gonna want to leave for the evening, okay? You already got what you wanted. Our deal is done. So... so go on, now." The deputy made a weak gesture with one of his hands.

More a limp-wristed, little flourish than anything particularly commanding.

And the gathered figures seemed to sense his hesitation. They all watched him, stoic and quiet.

The deputy tried to raise his voice, waving his hands again. "Come on now! This is our town—we respect the deal, you all gotta do the same. You get this once a month. We'll just reschedule, okay? So go on—git!"

The deputy had stepped back now, realizing a slow murmur was rising from the masked figures around him. He stumbled over a stone protrusion as he stepped back, his hand lingering on his holster, his eyes wide. "Come on, be reasonable! We don't need Feds in Parcel. Let's go. Git!"

Finally, the man standing in the water spoke. "Can you reschedule the sun?"

The deputy blinked, hesitated, opened his mouth to reply, but was cut off as if the leader in the water was waiting for this.

He spread his arms, his crimson sleeves catching the wind, a faint prickle of moisture along the soft fabric. The leader stepped forward, calling out, his voice echoing—the voice of someone used to oration. "Can you calm the breeze? Can you waylay the lightning storms? Can you watch the rain until you find its berth?"

The deputy blinked. "Shit man, I'm not into any of that. Just, go. Okay? I'm sure the sun would get you coming back a few days from now. The Feds will be out soon enough."

Brenner's hand lingered on his weapon, but Ella reached out, holding his wrist. She whispered, "Too many of them. They might be armed."

Brenner shrugged. "So what?" he replied quietly.

Ella's hand clenched tightly, her fingernails biting into her palm as she considered this very thing, confronted by the bizarre spectacle below.

At last, the deputy muttering a few more comments, panicked and afraid in nearly the same way the sheriff had been, the robed figures finally began to move. Two abreast, striding next to each other, they brushed past the deputy. The leader gestured them on, and they moved around the side of the white stone plateaus, moving up the mutli-level pools towards the mountains now.

All of the red figures followed the leader's wordless directions, his finger waving...

All of them except one.

A small, thin figure, lingering near the back. Up until this point, Ella had thought this figure was participating along with the rest. But now, she heard a shout. It was difficult to spot the origin of the sound, due to the face masks, but the figure was struggling now, bucking and trying to break free.

There was a flash under the sun, and Ella realized, stunned, that this smaller figure—a female figure by the looks of it—was *handcuffed* to a burly man at her side.

Chapter 14

Ella's stomach dropped. The handcuffed woman, concealed in the same robes and mask as the cultists around her, threw herself towards the deputy. She jerked to a halt as the tall, muscled figure she was bound to yanked on the cuffs, and she crumpled to her knees like a toddler seized by an irate adult. Another man stepped forward, snaring her other arm. Together, the large, burly figure and his backup dragged the protesting young woman away.

"No! Help me! Help me, please! NO! NO!"

The deputy just stared, wincing, looking terrified. The blood had drained from his face. He even opened his mouth as if to say something, staring as the figure was pushed forward by the two rough men. Now that Ella watched, she realized that one of the men was clearly carrying a pistol under his robe, its outline pressed to the fabric. The other figures, she noticed, staring, had similar telltale bulges.

The deputy just stared, forlorn. He muttered something, inaudible over the woman's screams and the sound of marching boots against white stone. But Ella thought it looked distinctly like the word, *sorry*.

Still, he didn't move to intervene.

Brenner on the other hand, did. Gun in hand, stepping forward now, passing the second row of trees, ready to emerge, but Ella caught his shoulder, yanking him back.

"No!" she whispered fiercely. "They're armed!"

He whirled to look at her, glaring. "They're hurting her!"

Now, the red figures were a hundred yards away, still dragging the protesting straggler behind them. Their leader, instead of marching with them, was *swimming* up the pool, rising—dripping sheets of water—to then move up the next pool. He clambered up the slick stone chute and followed a small stream, moving through the mist cast by the geysers and the heated water. Wherever he stepped, droplets of water speckled the stone behind him, tapping against the winking, glittering marble.

Ella breathed heavily, staring after the retreating figures. The deputy was leaning against the white shelf of rock at his side, a look of relief across his features. Perspiration, which had nothing to do with the steam, streamed down his face. And he used the colored bandanna to wipe at his countenance.

"Ella," Brenner hissed in her ear, "They're getting away."

"There's too many of them, Brenner," Ella shot back.

"God dammit! We can't call for backup, so we're all *she's* got. That might be the girl we came for!"

Ella was still staring, watching as the red-robed figures disappeared over the white stone, moving hastily away and back up towards the blue mountain.

"I know where they're going," Ella said at last, her voice low.

"How could you?"

"Helen mentioned it."

"Who?"

"There's another lake. Some sort of sacred lake, up in the mountains. That's where the deputy sent them. They'll be there."

Brenner was breathing more calmly now, staring at the side of her face. "We can't just sit here," he said, his voice a growl.

Ella's own heart was pounding. She felt fear pulsating through her system, and part of her wanted to join Brenner in a breakneck sprint up the slopes. Ella knew what it was to chase adrenaline, to cut loose and allow sheer will to direct her steps.

But she also knew what it was to stay reserved. To wait. To allow patience the first word.

Those figures were all armed. Even with Brenner, they were out-gunned. And the deputy was there too—judging by the way things had gone, he would've joined things on the side of the red-robed figures.

Now, as the group disappeared around the bluff, beneath one of the dark caves from which the underwater spring trickled, Brenner finally slumped full, rubbing a hand against his eyes. He breathed heavily, cursing as he did and shaking his head, his gun in his holster, his hand clutching it as if it were some sort of security blanket.

Ella didn't feel much better, but she knew talking wouldn't solve anything. There was another lake in those mountains. Abraham was supposedly back in town at a dance, and the Graveyard Killer was missing.

"It's all going to shit," Ella said, shaking her head and slamming a hand against the tree. Small flecks of bark and strands of wood fluttered past the abuse of her clenched fist.

"We should've helped her," Brenner said.

Ella gave a quick, certain shake of her head. This was the big difference between Ella and her sister. Priscilla had shot Zeke Chernow the previous day when he'd been charging with a knife towards a young woman. Ella had held her fire because she knew she might've hit an innocent bystander. Priscilla had charged into a blizzard, leading ten men into the freeze in search of their cousin.

Ella had gone as well but had taken a more cautious approach. Until the polar bear attack, that was.

Priscilla wore her heart on her sleeve and always operated with reckless abandon. Ella, though, used determination like any tool. Sometimes it was the right tool for the job, but other times a more tactful approach was needed.

And in this case...

She'd made the right call. Hadn't she? There had been too many...

Was she concerned about herself? About the screaming woman dragged away by those hooded folk?

Or about something else?

She glanced at Brenner, frowning.

But he was distracted now, staring at the ground with a frown on his face. "What the hell?" he muttered, bending slowly, his fingers scraping through the pine needles.

Ella watched as the ex-SEAL slowly plucked something off the forest floor, dislodging it from where it had wedged under a pine cone near a muddy, protruding root. Brenner raised it slowly, holding it up to catch the sunlight streaming through the thick foliage.

"Is that..." Ella leaned in, wrinkling her nose.

"A finger bone," Brenner murmured. He scuffed the fallen leaves, scraping moss from a root accidentally as he disheveled the ground cover. "There—more," he said, his voice shaking.

Ella stared. Indeed, multiple bones lay scattered amidst the fallen leaves. A couple more finger bones. A few teeth. What looked like part of a jaw, and other bits and pieces so old and decayed Ella couldn't quite discern what they were.

She stared at the ground, where the bones were scattered. Where was the rest of the skeleton, then? Only enough parts to fill a small cup lay scattered before them. Perhaps critters had come along and absconded with the rest.

Ella considered this but then shook her head. The bones were *very* old. The idea that those fingers, that jaw would've been left behind, allowed to remain clumped together for... what must have been years, maybe decades, seemed unlikely.

Unless, for some reason, wildlife hadn't had access to the bones. Perhaps someone watched the grove... She shot quick looks around, feeling a slow pins-and-needles sensation up her back.

But no one was in sight. Besides, the grove was large, and come nightfall, creatures could move unobstructed amidst their natural habitat.

So that meant that bones had only recently been placed here... Had someone discarded them? But no—some were on top of the oak leaves, some beneath. Some wedged in the mud, others—like a tooth Brenner was now holding up—resting on a root.

As if the bones had been sprinkled, slowly...

Or fallen.

She turned slowly, feeling as if her pounding heart might burst from her chest. She redirected her gaze, sweeping it up the massive, ancient oak Brenner had been leaning against. Ivy, moss, and thick bark all culminated in a canopy of deep green.

And then she went still.

"Brenner," she murmured.

"Look—I think this is a wedding ring."

"Brenner! Look!"

"What? I don't think—oh." Brenner went still, following her indicated finger.

The two of them stared up into the branches, both still. A wooden platform had been nailed into the branches, and some chickenwire was stretched between two-by-fours. The wood itself was rotten, clearly very old.

But there, seventy feet above them, resting on the makeshift stretcher of nailed two-by-fours and chickenwire, Ella's eyes landed on a human skeleton.

It lay motionless, in scattered pieces, crumbling away, and evidently, pieces falling through the chickenwire as the bones broke down. Or—perhaps—squirrels, possums and other night-time creatures disturbed the scaffold. By the look of things, at least one bird had made a nest up there.

Brenner whistled quietly under his breath, staring up... But then his eyes swept to the left, towards a smaller tree, and he said, "Ella!" sharply. "Ella, look!"

She turned and stared. Another platform. This one far fresher, made of new lumber and bright wire. The corpse was decayed but still had some skin, dried and blackened as it was.

"There!" Brenner said, pointing to another, even older tree. Another body on a makeshift platform far, far above the ground.

And as Ella glanced about, moving slowly, she spotted more bones amidst the leaves. Even one skeleton where it apparently had rolled off its elevated platform. As she moved through the horrifying graveyard grove, she spotted other things. Markings on the trees. Sometimes lower but other times halfway up or even further up the tree trunks. "Brenner—read that."

He did, leaning in, eyes narrowed. There, gouged into the wood, about a foot above Brenner's head, was a simple word. *Mary.* Then a number. *5*7.

"Think that's the names and ages?" Brenner asked.

But Ella shook her head in uncertainty, pointing to another tree. This time indicating gouge marks far, far higher up. She strained to read it, but it would have been impossible if Brenner hadn't pulled out his phone, aimed the camera and zoomed in.

The two of them stared at the screen of the cell without service.

The words were harder to make out, filled with sap and overgrown with moss. But the markings were wide and deep enough, scarring the bark, that Ella was able to discern the name. *"Johanna. 02."*

"Not ages," Ella said slowly. "That body isn't a child's." As she said it, she felt a flicker of disgust. But as she pointed towards the scaffold far, far up—almost a hundred feet in the air—affixed to the boughs of a sparse fir, a full-sized skeleton leered down at them. The rest of the body was missing. Either absconded with or turned to dust.

"I think..." Ella said, reading other numbers and names... "I think those numbers are burial dates."

"What?"

"Burial dates," she repeated. "Mary, 1957. Johanna, 1902. Which m eans... if that plane the Dawkins cult crashed landed here... there were others around these parts long before. Hell, maybe it was even some routine pilgrimage."

"1902? That was... more than a hundred and twenty years ago."

Ella nodded, feeling a shiver, but she pointed at a final, much smaller tree. This one had a corpse with clothing and skin still mostly maintained. Though decay had set in. "*Nina, 2021,*" Ella read quietly.

"That was this year," Brenner replied, taking a few shuffling steps back and avoiding the root obstacles pushed up from the ground. His voice carried equal parts awe and disdain. "God dammit, your creepy friend was right."

"He's not my friend," Ella murmured, turning one way then the other. "At least fifteen," she said.

"Bodies?"

"Yeah—I count fifteen."

"Shit... well that's not a good sign." Brenner had lowered his gaze towards the ground again, but now he was pointing off to their left.

Ella turned, frowning, and there she spotted something that sent shivers up her spine. A freshly made scaffold. Two-by-fours with bright, shiny chickenwire stretched between the beams. The scaffold hadn't been used yet but had been left leaning against the trunk of uniformly round oak. A few leaves had gathered on top of the scaffold where it leaned against the bark but not many.

"Looks new," Brenner said. "Thinking they might come back for that soon. This time with a passenger for it." He made a faint whistling sound, lifting a finger as if tracing a rocket taking off.

Ella nodded as well, scowling. She shot a look over her shoulder, back in the direction of town, then up the slopes where the young woman had been dragged. Did they dare wait for nightfall? Did the woman have that long?

"What's the call?" Brenner said, crossing his arms as he stepped back into a patch of sunlight under the canopy, giving himself not only warmth but also distance from having anything gory accidentally tumble on his head.

Ella tapped her foot against the ground, but then muttered. "We need backup to help that young woman."

"Backup *how,* Ella? The SAT phone with the heli might get us some static at best. No one's going to come out here, especially not as night falls."

"I know. Not that sort of backup."

"What sort?"

Ella patted a hand against her pocket, as if simply searching for the reassuring weight of the parchment held within. "Abraham," she said simply. "And Mortimer."

"Your CI gave me the slip."

"He's around here somewhere," she replied. "It was his idea to come looking for Rose."

"Who is he, really, Ella? Black ops?"

"Black... *what*? Is that what he said?"

"No. But he's not some low-rung CI."

Ella shook her head. "For now, he's our only backup. That's what. Abraham and Graves."

"We don't know whose side Abraham is on."

"We do," Ella said quietly. "And we know where he'll be, too. At a dance tonight. It's almost evening anyway. If we can find him, and find Graves, we can head up those slopes and find out what the hell is going on here."

Brenner shook his head. "She might not have that much time."

But Ella replied, "Do you think they're going to lug a corpse down a mountain?"

"What?"

Ella pointed at the branches. "They're going to put her body on that wire and raise her up. Chances are that means they'll kill her *here.*" She indicated the tree stump Brenner had spotted earlier with the stains and the gouge marks in it—it really *did* look like an altar.

"So you're saying you think she's safe until they bring her back down?"

"Safe, no. Alive, yes. Hopefully. We need backup. And then we need to go find this sacred lake of theirs and figure out what the hell is going on."

"Waiting for nightfall might be a mistake," Brenner shot back. "Darkness cuts both ways."

"Well... a fair fight puts us two against at least twenty."

"Who were those people?"

"I think we just met the Dawkins cult."

"Yeah... but... I thought the rumor was their plane crashed recently. Not..." he pointed to the tree with the highest gouge marks. "A hundred and twenty years ago."

Ella shrugged. "It might not have been the cult's first trip north, if you catch my drift. Hunting season is different depending on the prey."

"Shit. That's ominous."

Ella was turning now and moving quickly. Brenner fell into step.

It didn't feel good to put her back to a woman in need, her cries of desperation still lingering on the air. But as Ella picked up her pace, moving hastily back in the direction of Parcel, her stomach twisted with each step.

Even *with* backup, assuming they could find Graves and assuming Abraham was where the sheriff had said he'd be... and was willing to help... there was no saying how many of those red-cloaked figures were in the mountains. How many were armed. Or how many captives they had to begin with.

The sheriff and the deputy were clearly spooked. The people of Parcel were one thing... but those figures... they seemed a different sort. Ella wasn't sure what strange symbiotic relationship existed between the town and those cultists, but she knew that whatever was happening, it was costing lives.

And people *knew* about it. How couldn't they? Scaffolding in the trees, bodies there too... The townsfolk would've seen. Would've known. Tourists came through here as well, according to the sheriff.

But maybe that was the test...

Secrets had to be kept.

And the best way to choose one's next meal might easily be the same as deciding whose lips they needed sealed—permanently.

Tourists who stuck to the lake, safe enough.

But those who wandered too far afield? The next victim.

And Ella and Brenner had seen far, far more than they were supposed to have.

There was no backup for now, but another reason Ella wanted to head back to town was to grab the SAT phone in the heli and radio Nome. At least that way, she could let someone know where she was.

In case everything went sideways.

Brenner and Ella were jogging now, both of them moving side-by-side over the dusty trail, past the wooden fence outside the log home and heading back to town.

As they moved, the prickle of dread along Ella's spine only intensified.

They needed to be quick. Grab Abraham. Find Graves. Make the call on the SAT phone, then head back up that mountain to rescue the screaming woman.

What could possibly go wrong?

Chapter 15

By the time they reached the lake again, evening had come slowly. The sky continued to darken as Ella and Brenner moved hurriedly around the lake in the direction of the glowing lights. Ella had pictured some sort of dance hall, or maybe a tavern with an open floor for a hoe down.

What she hadn't been expecting was the small fleet of boats on the water, rocking and swaying gently, and the large inflatable, rectangular stage floating between the boats, anchored with chains so it wouldn't slip away.

Townies, young and old, were laughing, clapping and dancing excitedly on the inner-tube stage. Young men and women swirled about, arm in arm. Older men and women moved slower, but no less joyful for it.

Music came from an honest-to-goodness fiddle and banjo duo sitting in a small canoe, both of them with bare feet dangling in the water, straw hats tilted back on their excited faces.

At least a hundred people had gathered, and more were coming in. Some unhitching their boats from trolleys while others lowered their craft from the elevated platforms near personal docks.

The laughter echoed through the air, and glowing lantern light cast strange shadows across the water. The sound of mirth, music and joy contrasted sharply with the scene Ella had just left behind her.

Now, breathing heavily, about a half an hour of quick marching and hard jogging later, her eyes darted about the gathering, searching desperately.

Brenner breathed heavily at her side but then nodded towards one of the boats. "That him?"

She followed his gaze but then shook her head. "No—that's a scarf, not a bandage. Dammit—move this way. Come on—*this way.*"

Brenner noticed the source of her consternation. The sheriff was standing near the front of the dancing platform, leaning forward on the same fishing boat he'd been out in earlier. He laughed and clapped, cheering and whooping at the dancers as the tempo of the music picked up. His face was somewhat red, and the large paper bag containing a bottle inside his boat gave evidence to the reason for his good mood.

"No go," Brenner said suddenly, catching her arm and pulling. Ella stumbled against him but turned sharply, noticing his indicating finger.

Two other familiar figures were lingering on a dock extending from the shore only fifty feet ahead of them. The townies Brenner had beaten up. They were with the sheriff's daughter again, but there was no sign of the young woman who Brenner had sent running.

Ella felt a flicker of unease. They had to hurry. The woman who'd been taken to the mountains didn't have time for them to waste. So where the hell was—

"Lovely evening, isn't it?"

She turned sharply, Brenner as well.

Mortimer Graves appeared behind them, like a wraith. She felt certain he hadn't been there before. But he wasn't breathing heavily, nor did he look disheveled. Immaculate as ever, he adjusted his sleeves, and smiled at the two of them—the glimmer didn't quite reach his eyes.

"Where have you been?" Ella demanded, her voice on edge.

He watched her with his hollow gaze. "Finding our fair-headed vanishing act."

"Excuse me?"

"Now, Eleanor, this really isn't becoming of you. Normally, you're so reserved. I thought we *wanted* to interview the ever-elusive Abraham."

Ella went still, staring. "You have him?" she whispered.

"Hey! Hey, you!" a voice called out from by the lake. Larry, the tough guy who Brenner had hit, was glaring at them, red-faced, pushing to his feet, though his legs were wobbly.

The boat rocked beneath him, swaying from his stumbling stance. Ella flinched and began prodding at her two companions, pushing them back up towards the tree line, past the nearest log home facing the lake.

"I do indeed," said Mortimer with a thin-lipped smile. "If you ask kindly, I'll happily make introductions."

Larry, on the boat, was now trying to shout over the music. "Sheriff! Sheriff—they're back! Right there!"

Ella double-timed after Mortimer, and he led the lot of them through the trees. A couple of times Brenner tried to grab at the suited man's arm, but he slipped free, marching on ahead, ignoring Ella's hissing for him to slow.

"Graves," she said, her voice tense, "Wait—wait, slow down. Where's Abraham?"

But he simply pointed through the woods, and she realized he was directing them towards the small motel cabin they'd been shown to earlier.

The sound of Larry's yelling faded, the music over the lake swelling, the dancing feet and laughter increasing in tempo. As they moved behind the wooden home, Ella's sidelong glances found movement along the water, flickering lights reflecting off the placid lake, occasionally disturbed by wakeless boats and insistent paddles.

"Here we are, now..." Graves paused, turning, one hand braced against the wooden door of the small motel. He looked at Brenner and Ella in turn. "Don't do anything... rash," he said quietly.

Then, he fiddled with the latch, inserting a key—which Ella dreaded finding out how he had procured—then he opened the door with a faint *creak*.

She cast a glance along the side of the motel, towards the muddy terrain where Abraham had first spotted her, clearing the footprints.

She wanted to linger, to consider, to *think*. But time was of the essence. They'd come for backup. They needed help. Abraham would be that help but also their linchpin. The answer to everything. Or so she hoped.

And so it was with some shock that, as she pushed into the small space, she spotted the handsome, blond, young man tied to a chair. His white bandages along the side of his face still bulging against his head. His eyes wide with fear; his nostrils flaring.

When he spotted the three of them filing into the room, he let out a faint whimper.

"What the hell," Brenner muttered coldly.

But Graves shut the door behind them with a sweep of his foot. The door *clicked* shut. And for a brief moment, the light from outside was quelled. The only illumination came from the glow of Brenner's phone. Then a faint *click*.

A small penlight in Graves' hand, which he shone towards Abraham.

"He was the little perv in the rafters," Graves said quietly. "He knew about the hiding spot. I found an Abraham shaped clearing in the dust. He's up to his neck in all of this."

Abraham was still whimpering, a gag shoved in his mouth. The gag was familiar to Ella. The same pattern she'd seen on the bandanna in the deputy's belt. She frowned as Graves approached Abraham and held a knuckle to his lips.

"Remember now," Mortimer chided in a would-be gentle tone, like a mother assuaging a storm-frightened child. "What happens if you scream."

Abraham's eyes flared in terror again, but he nodded rapidly, breathing in quick puffs.

Then, Mortimer Graves plucked the gag from his mouth, patted Abe on the head, smoothing his hair kindly to the side, away from the injured portion of his face. "Now tell them what you told me," Graves said slowly. "And leave nothing out."

Abe let out a shaking breath. He stared at them all, still tightly bound to his chair. His tongue darted out, licking his lips. Then, breathing heavily, he whispered, "Are you... are you really here to rescue Rose?"

Ella was moving quickly. Time was ticking. She pulled the notes from her pocket, listening as they crinkled. She waved them at Abe. "Did you write these?"

He stared, blinked a few times, then Graves adjusted the beam of the light, illuminating the paper. His eyes widened, and he nodded. "Y-yes," he stammered. "To..." he swallowed. "To her. I'm not a perv!" he added quickly, frowning at Graves.

Ella pointed at the attic. She didn't linger long on wondering *how* Graves had elicited a confession. But at least Abraham didn't look injured... save the injury he'd already possessed when she'd first stumbled on him. "What's the creepy crawl space for," she said softly, keeping her tone even, her expression neutral, curious rather than frightened and angry.

"I... I..." he mumbled. "I'm supposed to make sure the outsiders are..." a swallow. "Safe," he whispered.

"Safe? Safe how?" Ella asked.

Abraham's eyes darted to the side, then back again. He winced. "I... I didn't mean to spy."

"Oh, come now," Graves said warmly. "A pretty young woman like Rose? Unsuspecting?"

Abe hastily shook his head. "I never watched anything indecent!" he declared, leaning back, his arms straining from his bonds. "I swear I didn't. It wasn't allowed. My mother would've... would've hurt me..." he winced, trailing off, his eyes darting in the opposite direction from where his bandages bulged.

"So you hid in the attic, watching... any tourist?"

He nodded quickly. "My family has to."

"Back up," Brenner cut in. "Your family?"

"My father, mother and me. We... we're told to, umm... Look, are we going to help Rose? They're going to do it at midnight."

"Do what?" Ella said sharply.

The blonde, young man looked at her. He hesitated, frowned, meeting her gaze, then murmured. "I think you know."

"Kill her?" Ella asked. "Hang her in one of those trees?"

Abraham winced. "You saw that?"

Brenner stepped in now, lifting his foot and pressing it against the chair, the wood creaking slightly as Brenner leaned in, studying Abraham's face. His foot was between the young man's legs, pushed against the frame of the seat for now, but the threat was evident. "So you stalk young women here, then pawn them off so others kill them?"

"No!" Abraham protested. "No—no! No one in town kills anyone. That's... we wouldn't. I just..." He winced. "I have to clean up. My family—the elders needed cleaners. It pays well. I dunno. Just... Rose was different. And I..." He stuttered, stammering and shaking his head. He seemed eager to share, to speak. But just as nervous.

His eyes kept darting to the door behind them all. Then his gaze would flick back, and he'd flinch, breathing shakily.

Ella said, slowly, "Cleaners? Elders? Are you members of the Dawkins cult?"

"No!" Abraham said sharply, his eyes wide. "No—not at all. None of us... those... those weirdos live in the mountains."

"In the red hoods," Ella said quietly.

"Y-yes," he said. Now, his voice was high-pitched, shaking. The fear was evident in his voice. "I... I never wanted to hurt anyone," he said quickly. "But... but if we didn't give them someone, they took two of us. It's the deal. It's always been the deal."

Graves was shaking his head now, scowling. "And my private investigator? Amanda? Tell them what you said about her."

"O-oh..." Abraham looked flustered, his cheeks turning red. Tears seemed to be welling in his eyes. "I didn't know what they were doing. I swear I didn't. I..."

"Tell them," Graves said, his voice cold and unrelenting.

"I... she came through a few weeks ago. I remember her," said Abraham quickly. "She was nice. But strange. I was watching her." He pointed to the ceiling. "I heard her make a call."

"That was to me," Graves said coldly. "And then what did you do, Abraham?"

"I just told the sheriff! Like I'm supposed to. I told him she was probably law enforcement and was snooping around. She disappeared the next day."

"Disappeared," Graves said. "And the deputy so happened to have the bandanna I gave her with the GPS chip sewn into the hem." Mortimer reached out, plucking the gag from where it dangled around Abraham's neck and then using it to wipe some of the sweat from the boy's features. He did it slowly, deliberately, and Abraham's eyes kept track of every motion, every flick of the wrist. His panic was evident.

"Sh-she..." Abraham stammered, panicked. "She's probably fine. Like Rose!"

"She's probably dead," Brenner said, cold. "We found a grove of trees, Mortimer," he said softly.

"Filled with bodies on platforms, I know," said Graves. He patted Abraham on the cheek. "The townies don't go out that way, do they? They're forbidden from the hot springs. If they stay here, stay with their own, leaving well enough alone, they're left unharmed..." His voice was like a purr, or like the low rumble of a motorcycle. He said, "My private investigator was supposed to brief me on everything she'd found... and then she went missing. Only a few weeks later, Rose Lewis, a young woman whose mother was searching high and low for her daughter, went missing." He sighed slowly, straightening, his average features creased into a frown. "What a shock it was to me," he murmured, "To find out just how *many* have gone missing."

Ella shot the serial killer a strange look. He'd hired a private investigator to look into the town *before* Rose Lewis' disappearance? Why?

He was clearly a man of means, a man with money and helicopters and contacts. He knew about Rose Lewis' mother somehow.

She wanted to ask more, to hurry, but mostly, she needed to know if Abraham could be trusted. They needed a fourth. She was already shaky on Graves, but having more backup she couldn't rely on might get her and Brenner killed.

But if they tarried too long, Rose would be killed.

Abraham was crying now, shaking his head. "I didn't know they were dying. I didn't, I swear. But—but I was just doing what I was told. Helping the town!"

"And what about Rose?" Ella asked, raising the letters again, the yellowed parchment casting a sickly pallor across her fingers thanks to the penlight.

"I... I liked her," he said softly. "We fell in love." He fidgeted uncomfortably as the young and restless were warrant to do when discussing their feelings. But his fear was greater than his shame. "We were going to get married! We wanted to start a family. It's this place—this... Parcel! Things don't change much here. Not really. But it's... it's my home!"

"And what about this?" Graves said quietly. He reached out, peeling back the bandage over Abraham's ear.

The young man winced and cursed as it was pulled down, but Graves held it low so the others could see, some of the tape used to adhere it to the side of his head had been ripped, but mostly, the bandage was left intact.

The ear, on the other hand, wasn't nearly so fortunate.

Ella gaped. The top half of the ear was missing, completely severed. By the look of things, the cut had been quick. Now, the ear was starting to heal, but it was a slow process, the missing portion of skin and cartilage being covered by scar tissue.

Abraham winced as Graves pressed the bandage back, patting the young man on the side of the head until he yelped.

Abraham hissed, "I—I was found helping Rose! They knew I was helping an outsider. I told her about... about..." he stammered, glancing off, staring at the ground.

"You're in it now, kid," Brenner said. "Might as well go the whole way."

Abraham looked up, his eyes still shimmering and burdened. "They found out I told Rose about the sacred lake. They took her. And... and I think she must've told them about me. About us. My mother had to..." He shook his head, hyperventilating now. "My parents are cleaners. They take care of the town's problems. So my mother had to..." he trailed off, his face white.

"Your mother, Helen, did that?" Ella asked, pointing.

Abraham stared at her with wide-eyed panic, very much like a deer in the headlights. But he nodded a single time, exhaling in a whimper. "We... we dispose of their things," he said quietly. "My father does. Suitcases, clothing. Luggage. We dump it down the well, cover it with stones. He's done it for so many... even before I was born!"

"You get rid of your victims' clothing," said Brenner. "So the whole town is part of this?"

"No!" Abraham said. "I swear it. Really. I know you don't believe me. But most people don't know. We really do stick to the lake. We don't go past the grove. Most don't know about the bodies. Most, even if they did, would never talk about it. Pretend they hadn't seen. The hot springs are off-limits because of... of *them.*"

"The Dawkins cult?"

"We know them as the Children of the Springs," Abraham muttered. "They're dangerous. Very dangerous. Growing up, we're all warned about them." He raised his voice and in a mocking tone, intonated, "*Do your homework, or the Spring Children will sneak through your window!*" He shook his head fiercely. "We don't go to the mountains. We don't visit the sacred lake except in the mornings. I told Rose not to go at night! I told her!" he sobbed now.

Ella and Brenner both shared a look. Graves watched the sobbing young man dispassionately, adjusting his cuff links, and standing quietly off to the side, with a look like a disapproving headmaster.

"We gotta get going," Brenner muttered. "Those ATVs they mentioned?"

Abraham inhaled shakily, perking up. "I know where they're kept! Everyone's at the lake—I can take you to them, just... just don't..."

"Leave you here with him?" Brenner guessed, nodding to Graves.

Abraham winced. Mortimer didn't blink, staring like a lidless adder in tall grass.

Ella had to make a decision. Abraham was clearly involved in all of this. Some sort of sneak thief in the attic, a peeping Tom keeping his eye on unsuspecting tourists. For what? *Why?* It still wasn't clear.

Some sort of offering to these Spring Children. This mountain cult. The fear in the sheriff's eyes was still fresh in her mind.

They knew about the cult, and it terrified them. They avoided them...

But women were dying. She didn't believe Abraham that the others in town didn't know about the grove. It was a good twenty or more miles from the lake itself, but there wasn't much to do in Parcel, was there, except explore. But the idea that no one talked about it? Pretended it was nothing?

This made sense to her.

The worst atrocities in history had been committed just outside the borders of some small town, where the residents swore they'd never heard a thing. Never seen a thing.

Intentional blindness, in Ella's estimation. But they were out of time. Rose was in danger. She'd gone up this mountain to this sacred lake. Like some sort of offering. A scapegoat, perhaps. She even pictured the deputy, shouting at the cultists in the springs.

The deputy had been terrified too. But he'd mentioned the *deal,* some arrangement between the town and the Spring Children. Abraham's father disposed of the tourists' private possessions. Abraham's mother had cut her own son's ear for breaking tradition.

There were some in the town far *less* innocent and naive than Abraham wanted to pretend.

But as for his love of Rose Lewis?

This she believed.

Twine wrapped in twine, wrapped in wire. Untangling this strange mess was causing her mind to ache. But Abraham would have to do.

If not, they would be too severely outnumbered.

And so, having been forced into trusting Graves on one side, she turned to Abraham and said, "You're coming with us. Brenner," she snapped her fingers. "Please," she added. "Knife."

The lanky marshal stepped forward, his pocket-knife springing out instantly and pressing to the ropes. Ella exhaled shakily, but then said, with more confidence than she felt, "We need to grab those ATVs. Then Brenner will give Graves his backup sidearm, and..."

"No need," Graves said quietly. "I have my own weapon." He patted his hip where a barely visible outline could be seen.

For some reason, the thought that Graves was armed only sent shivers up Ella's spine. But they were in it now, like Brenner had said. Might as well go all in. As the ropes fell, tumbling and unspooling around Abraham, Brenner cutting him free, Ella said, "The sidearm can go to Abe, then. Do you know how to shoot?"

He nodded warily.

"We're going to rescue Rose. But for that to happen, I need to know I can trust you."

"You can!" he exclaimed. "I love her! It's... it's the only thing that matters."

She stared at him, and he stared back. His eyes were bright, earnest, tear-filled and desperate. She found herself believing him.

And so she sighed, nodded, then gestured. "First, lead us to those ATVs. Come on—we need to go *now*."

Chapter 16

The all-terrain vehicle grumbled under her, shaking and growling as it moved back up the trail, kicking up streams of dust. Ella held her hands against Brenner's waist, gripping tight. Their path on the old, rusted, green four-wheeler was illuminated, their shadow stretching across the dirt in front of them, by the light of the second stolen ATV behind them.

According to the sheriff, only two vehicles had been available to the lake town. Ella hoped with the music, the noise, the town wouldn't realize their transportation was missing.

She shot a quick glance back, wind whipping about her, hair fluttering.

The strangely tepid air in the equally odd valley gusted over her, brushing at her skin. Her hands gripped Brenner where he prompted them forward. The faster they went, the more recklessly they sped away from the lake, the more at ease Ella felt.

Something about the adrenaline rush of an untrammeled expedition had always given Ella a second wind. So often, she held back thoughts, emotions. Instead of wearing her heart on her sleeve, she kept it buried deep, revealed only when useful.

But high speeds and dangerous choices had a way of releasing some of this pent-up repression.

And now, she felt fear melting, her smile widening, as they pushed faster and faster along the trail. Abraham had provided directions for a path he'd heard of that led up the side of the mountain to this sacred lake.

Now, they passed by the graveyard grove. No sign of light or motion or movement. Ella hoped this meant that Rose Lewis was still safe.

"Faster!" she shouted in Brenner's ear. "Faster if you can!"

He turned back, yelling at her. But she couldn't hear him over the sound of the engine and the wind. Then again, he yelled, but this time added a gesture: His thumb jutting past them, over his shoulder, indicating the ATV behind them.

She glanced back. Mortimer and Abraham were lagging. Falling further and further behind. Graves was driving, and he struck Ella as something of a more reserved, cautious man. He liked to plan and think long, long before making a move.

She still wasn't sure exactly *what* move he was making. Why he'd come to her, why he was involved in this at all. He killed killers. That seemed to be enough for him.

But it wasn't enough of an explanation for her.

She gripped Brenner's waist, feeling her eyes narrow in frustration as they slowed, allowing the second ATV to catch up.

Now, they were moving up the base of the mountain. Off to the right, as darkness continued to fall and night made itself known, Ella managed to glimpse spurts of steam rising from the many opaque pools in the white marble basins.

The headlights from the ATVs cut through the rising steam, glowing off the particles of moisture.

As she peered up the mountain, there was still no sign of the red-cloaked figures. No sign of *anyone.* She shivered, wondering if, even now, they were being watched. If their approach was noticed.

The town was scared of the cult in the mountains. And the Spring Children preyed upon the town, on the offerings provided by it. The unsuspecting tourists that came through—many made it out. But, clearly, many didn't.

Don't leave the lake. Don't intrude on the hot springs... it was something of a test, she supposed. It was why they'd hidden Abraham in the rafters of the motel. Why they kept an eye on tourists. To prevent anyone from wandering too far afield. She pictured the way the sheriff had continually attempted to corral her *back* towards town.

She didn't understand this place, but what little she had learned sent shivers up her spine. Now, as they slowed, rounding up the valley, inclining towards the peak of the blue mountain—Mount Sherman—Ella's eyes remained fixed on the jagged slopes, the switchbacks, the peaks. Desperately searching for anything untoward.

Abraham was shouting something behind them, waving his arm. Brenner glanced back, as did Ella. The young man was pointing off to the right. A small slope in the road led through a crevice in the rock she might not have noticed if not for Abraham's waving.

For someone who claimed they didn't venture up this way, he certainly knew a lot about the terrain.

Now, Brenner was forced to slow even further. She could hear her own breathing as they rumbled through the shadows, through the crevice. And then... they were forced to a stop, the trail turning to dense undergrowth and rocky-strewn slopes in front of them.

Brenner killed the engine. The second ATV approached from behind, came to a stop, and also died.

And for a moment, all of them sat in silence, breathing heavily, listening to the sounds of one another inhaling, exhaling.

And then Abraham's voice shook. "The lake is up ahead."

"I thought you didn't come this way," Ella said, frowning at him.

Abraham winced. "I—I don't. Just... when I was twelve. On a dare."

She stared at him, still uncertain if she could trust him in any way. Or, perhaps, worse... she knew she couldn't. Same as Graves. Two members of the supposed backup were untrustworthy and dangerous.

Abraham winced, shrugged and scratched at the bandage adhered to his face.

She shook her head, let out a huff and then hopped off the ATV, patting a hand against her holster, if only to double-check it was still there.

Brenner dismounted as well. And eventually, the four of them stood by the quiet machines, peering up the slope. Abraham was hesitant now. "I... I could've sworn this was the way. I think it changed."

"Since you've been here last, you mean?" Graves said, watching Abraham like a shark eyeing a sleeping seal.

"Mhmm," Abe took a step away from Graves even as he nodded uncomfortably.

But then, Brenner—who'd been scanning the undergrowth—grunted once, pointed and took off with that lanky stride of his, marching forward and gesturing for the others to follow.

Ella's frown only deepened as Brenner led them through the undergrowth, brushing aside branches and thorny bushes with mountain berries, the twigs snagging at her clothing.

She moved behind the taller man, watching as he managed to navigate a hidden trail carved through the undergrowth.

Ahead, she spotted the glow of the rising moon, reflecting off a glassy surface. Glimpses and glimmers of water attracted her gaze.

The lake ahead, she realized, was smaller than the one in Parcel. And now, she heard the faint sound of humming.

A buzzing murmur of softly spoken voices. She listened, the sound itching in her ears. Brenner slowed, and she followed suit. The two of them peered through the branches, their eyes on the wooden dock extending out to the lake.

A chain blocked the entrance to the dock, with a white-painted *Forbidden* sign dangling from the links. Thick tree roots jutted from the shore, into the water like enormous, woody arms scooping the liquid.

And now, as she kept low, against the tree cover, moving up a slight divot in the slanted ground, she heard the sound of the voices increasing in volume. A familiar chant—the same sounds they'd heard from the crimson-garbed Spring Children back at the base of Mount Sherman.

"From the earth. From the moon. From the heart. From the womb," they all chanted softly.

Ella spotted shadows on the opposite shore. Thirty figures at least, now. More than had been in the hot springs. Her heart pounded, rattling her bones, and her eyes fixated on the moon-soaked, blue-lit cloaked figures. They still wore their masks, save one man who was standing on the forbidden dock. His head was thrown back, his mask lowered.

He spoke in the same voice he'd used back at the base of the mountain, but now she realized it was a deeper, more booming voice than the one he'd used while tending the general store.

With his mask removed, hood thrown back, the man had the same friendly face, the same big, googly glasses that emphasized the color of his eyes, and he wore one of the beaded, blue-and-red necklaces she'd spotted back at his general store. He looked middle-aged and unremarkable, save his body fat percentage visible in the taper of his jaw and those pronounced cheekbones.

He was smiling at those gathered, his arms extended, his sleeves drooping like ruddy leaves fluttering above the still waters.

His voice echoed. "Brothers, sisters, this is our harvest."

The chanting voices went quiet, watching their leader. Dawson Kinsey was the name he'd given back at the general store. But now, as she stared, Ella was able to think for a moment. No longer confronted by the strange smells and sights of the new town, nor watched by residents who were all just a bit *too* attentive. She realized, now, that as she stared at Dawson Kinsey... the authority he seemed to have... the way his voice almost *changed* as he spoke. Not the genial, comforting and accommodating tone he'd used back in his general store by the helipad, but an older, more foreboding voice...

She wondered if something else had changed too.

That name.

Dawson Kinsey the Third, he'd said.

The cult they were looking for had been led by a man named Soney Dawkins. Dawson Kinsey.

The same letters. Was this man, hands-outstretched a son... a grandson? She didn't know how old Soney Dawkins had been on that plane which had made its fated crash-landing in the wilderness of Alaska all those years ago.

But now she suspected she was staring at Dawkins. The leader of the strange group.

"Shit," Brenner whispered, going suddenly still where he crouched on the shoreline opposite the cultists.

Ella spotted the source of his consternation. Figures were stepping forward now, their arms raised, bare. Knives in their off hands. The chanting continued again, and over the slow, steady chants, Dawkins was calling out, "In the way of the wild, it's those who risk that yield fruit. A gentle answer invites wrath—but a strong hand guides the flock!"

The chanting continued. "From the earth! From the heart!"

The knives pressed against the bare skin, and Ella spotted scars on the wrists over the water. The leader of the cult called out. "And do you, my dear children, accept the cost to be born in water and of blood?"

Laughter from some of the others gathered. Faint clapping.

The five figures with knives pressed to their arms all nodded. They then—one at a time—drew blood. Their arms shot out over the lake, and blood droplets tapped into the liquid, sending out the faintest ripples with hearts of crimson.

A silence suddenly descended as everyone stared at the pattering blood drops. The quiet hung over the lake. The mountain wind gusted down, chillier than the air in the valley.

Ella found herself shivering, her hand resting on her weapon, feeling the comforting grip, the cold metal chilly against her fingertips.

As the five arms spread over the water, the leader of the group called out, "Now join your brethren, seen and unseen. Countenances turned to those of kin and ken."

Following this strange and garbled cue, all five figures bleeding into the water removed their hoods. Ella stared, heart in her throat.

She recognized the deputy with the pinched face. The same man who'd warned the cult to leave the hot springs. She recognized Mrs. Puzo, the motel-keeper. Three others she didn't quite recognize. Though a couple she seemed to recall from glimpses around town back in Parcel.

Abraham was trembling where he rested against the ground, staring directly at the man on the far left of the five new recruits. This man's arm extended, bleeding. He had the same blond hair as Abraham and similar features. He wasn't quite as handsome, not just a product of his age, but from the way his face seemed to droop, wrinkled and worn and weathered.

"Dad..." Abraham whispered, his voice trembling. "Th-that's my dad. Dad... DA—"

He tried to shout out, the outburst cutting through the night before Mortimer clapped a hand over his lips and pressed him to a tree, growling in the boy's ear.

But the damage had been done.

The man she supposed was Dawkins whirled about on the dock, staring towards the trees. A few of the gathered figures on the shore, wearing their long, flowing red robes, also looked over. But most didn't seem to notice. Either chanting or murmuring to each other.

Abraham's father, a cleaner like his wife, according to his son, glanced off into the trees, a look of surprise and then fear in his eyes. He masked the look quickly, though.

Mortimer kept his hand pressed tightly to Abraham's face, holding back any further shouts.

The silence fell over the clearing again. Eyes searched the trees, figures stared towards where they were hiding. Ella remained motionless, crouched, hidden in both undergrowth and shadow.

Brenner had gone still as stone at her side.

After a bit, Dawkins began breathing easier again, but his eyes were still narrowed and his lips pressed in a thin line. His jovial eyes, behind those googly glasses, were also pressed tight, his brow furrowed and ridged.

He made a gesture, and three of the cultists, standing further back, began to move. Ella glimpsed weapons in their hands as they slipped off through the trees, disappearing from the shore, and likely moving to some path.

A path, she guessed, which would lead to *them.*

"We need to move," she whispered to Brenner.

He was beginning to nod in agreement. As Ella tried to rise, to slip back, another commotion caught her attention.

Dawkins had raised a hand, gesturing towards the tree line, calling out, "Bring her!"

Suddenly, there was shouting. Desperate pleading. "Please! Please don't!" the voice shook. "I'm begging you, please! I don't know anything. I don't! I didn't mean to!"

Ella had gone still again. She stared towards where the ranks of the red figures parted, and a new, bucking and thrashing and kicking young woman was brought into the mix.

The five bleeding recruits on the shore still gripped their knives, staring, the water placid at their backs, their blood having soaked into the basin.

Three large, strong men were shoving the small, frail young woman forward. Ella's hackles went up seeing the way they mistreated her. Twice her size, each of the men took turns dragging her, pushing or shoving her. One jolted her so hard, she hit the ground. Then another

198

yanked her up by her hair—which elicited a shout of pain—and pulled her further.

She was still wearing a red cloak but no mask now.

The woman's eyes were wide with fright. Young and tan with loose, curly hair, the girl's eyes were full of terror.

Mortimer Graves, sensing the moment, had directed Abraham's eyes towards her. They bugged, and he was nodding. But it was Graves who whispered, loud enough for them to hear, "Rose Lewis."

Ella felt tingles along her arms and her spine.

The girl was being shoved towards the shore. Eventually, the three thugs guiding her, they gave her a huge push. She stumbled forward; tripped; barely caught herself, hand scraping through mud and small branches; and her feet splashed in the shallows. Judging by her sudden tensing, the water was cold.

Off to their right, Ella heard movement now. Voices. The sound of the three scouts Dawkins had sent around the lake to investigate the noise. The three armed men were making their way towards the hiding spot.

But Ella froze in place now, staring across the water. Her teeth pressed tightly together. They were outnumbered.

Rose Lewis was sobbing, pleading. The five townies with knives and bleeding arms were moving towards her.

Dawkins shouted, "The trade is made. Five from Parcel joins our kin, and we offer one soul in sacrifice."

"The deal is struck!" called out the deputy, Abraham's father, Mrs. Puzo and the others.

"Please!" Rose yelled.

Abraham was still pressed to the tree, Graves' fingers clasped over his face, holding back any further shouts. But the look of terror in his eyes, of fear, sent chills through Ella's heart.

They were pressing Rose back now, pushing her into the lake, knives in hand as the five recruits shepherded her into the water.

Ella had thought they'd do the killing back in the grove... but now she realized, in horror, she'd been mistaken.

They were about to murder Rose Lewis. Thirty of the red-cloaked figures. Only four of them.

Three men only twenty paces or so away, stomping through the undergrowth, circling the water.

Ella wanted to scream, wanted to raise her gun and fire. But if she did, it would elicit return fire. For all she knew, the rest of them would perish and Rose too.

But she couldn't do *nothing*.

Brenner was trying to pull at her, his own eyes darting between Rose's inevitable fate—she'd stumbled again, now knee-deep in the cold lake, desperately pleading. The knife-wielders, five paces away, encroaching, bloody blades extended.

But Brenner also kept glancing in the direction of the approaching voices. The trudging feet.

Ella reached a decision. She pressed her weapon against Brenner's chest. "Keep low—don't get seen until Rose is clear!"

"What are you—"

But she didn't wait to discuss it.

No time.

Rose was now waist deep. They would stab her or drown her, and they didn't seem to care which. All eyes were fixated on her now. Dawkins' too.

And so Ella left her weapon against Brenner's chest—it would be no use to her. And then she broke from the tree cover.

Brenner cursed, tried to snag her arm.

Missed.

She darted out under the moon, onto the muddy shore. Her pulse pounded. Her heart leapt in her throat. Two steps. Three. Prints in the soft earth.

Someone could see her. Someone might shout. Someone might *shoot*.

And then she reached the water. Quiet, swift, she slipped into the frigid liquid, slipping under the sacred lake and using the still water as a glassy cover for her. As the water swelled around her, freezing and cold, and as she inhaled deeply, drawing air into her lungs, her head finally dipped under the liquid as well.

And no one spotted her. The pack of ravenous wolves were all too focused on their prey, cornering her, the five knives flashing. Rose shouted, splashing as she stumbled back. Up to her chest now, soaking and shivering and pleading.

The sounds behind her faded—she hoped Brenner knew what to do.

The sounds ahead of her increased in volume. Chanting, laughter, the screams of their victim.

And then the lake swallowed her. She dipped under, into, down, down, down. The darkness pressed in around her. The faint smear of white, the interference of the moon, served as her anchoring point, her directing compass.

And she swam, eyes straining, mildly stinging from the cold. The water pressing around her, soaking her instantly, saturating her hair, flowing across her form. She kicked, trying not to move swiftly but quietly.

She went low—lower than she might otherwise have gone, terrified that someone on the shore would spot her.

She swam—fast. Kicking and picking up pace.

She didn't look back, didn't reconsider. The same way Priscilla had marched into a blizzard, indifferent to the threat, Ella now cut through the water, moving rapidly, silently and stealthily towards where Rose was stumbling.

The smaller lake was still larger than a pool. Much larger. But Ella could hold her breath—she'd proven it before in freezing ice water.

Bubbles trickled past her cheeks. Her blood pounded in her ears.

And she swam. Moving rapidly, five feet under the surface, the moon as guidance, cutting towards where Rose Lewis was about to be murdered.

Chapter 17

Brenner stared, stunned, horror in his heart as he stared at the ripple where Ella had slipped into the lake, swimming underwater towards the poor, young woman crying for help.

He gripped Ella's sidearm in one hand. His mind raced rapidly. He couldn't let Ella go at it alone. There were too many.

"God dammit," he whispered to himself. Part of him wanted to bolt after her, to follow her into the water and then...

Then what?

What was her *plan*?

He hissed sharply, feeling a rising sense of indignation and fury. But another hiss caught his attention. Mortimer Graves, staring at him, those cold, reptile eyes peering over his shoulder. His corpse-like hands were still pressed to Abraham's mouth, holding back a scream.

But now, Graves was watching Brenner and jerking his head to the side.

Brenner had heard them too.

Three gunmen, now converging on their hiding spot. By the quiet muttering, the crunch of leaves and twigs, Brenner guessed the gunmen hadn't spotted the three trespassers.

But Ella had been clear. They needed to be kept quiet.

She'd wanted them to run, to hide.

But Brenner wasn't the running sort. He pointed at Abraham, held a finger to his lips, then pointed at Graves and raised an eyebrow. A question.

A look passed between the two men, both of them staring at the other. Neither of them much liked what they saw. It was something in the DNA—something in Brenner's bones that felt cold whenever he was around Ella's CI.

But he also knew a killer when he saw one.

This particular, reptile-eyed killer was smiling now. He slowly lowered his hand, whispering something in Abraham's ear. The boy was hyperventilating but no longer screaming. After the whisper, Abraham, face pale and panicked, slipped down the tree, dislodging fragments of bark as he slowly gathered his legs under him in a huddle. The ferns at his side swished by his face, and Abraham twitched, trembling and terrified. His one hand moved up, touching daintily at his bandaged ear.

But now, Graves was moving. The look between the men was over, but they'd reached an understanding.

Neither of them, it would seem, was the running sort.

"Think it was this way!" one of the voices was saying, moving slowly forward. Brenner watched the dark shapes of three, red-cloaked figures finally push into the clearing.

And he dove to the ground, using the ferns, the undergrowth and the thick roots as cover. He went still, inhaling earth, embracing mud.

"Ah, shit," another said, "nothing here. It's just the forest."

"Brother Damon—the sun cleanse your lips!"

"Ah—damn. Yeah. Sorry. I mean... dang..."

The voices drifted off into muttering. Three shadows moved past Brenner. One of them stepped within five feet, pausing briefly. The other two circled around either side of the tree where Abraham was leaning back, frozen in place. Two more steps and these second two would spot the young man.

No sign of Graves.

How the hell did he do that?

Brenner didn't flinch, though—didn't move. He remained quiet, pressed to the earth, listening.

The man above him, five paces away, was staring across the lake, watching the strange scene beyond. The gunman had a pistol in one hand, which still had its safety on and was pointed at the earth.

The two other men were flanking the tree Abraham was using for cover, both were speaking louder now, bickering about one man's "potty mouth."

One pace before they spotted Abraham.

No choice.

Brenner moved.

Instead of going after the man facing the lake, though—the man closest to him—he surged to his feet, a blur of shadow, and charged the two men near Abraham.

He'd timed it perfectly.

Waiting for them to step forward. To spot Abraham. To turn sharply, both distracted. And then Brenner lunged. One gunman, pistol at the ground, safety on, facing the lake and watching the murder. This man's back was to Brenner.

The other two turned sideways, distracted by Abraham. They didn't spot him either.

Brenner covered the four paces in a split second, knife in hand. He jammed it into the throat of the man with the "unclean lips" as the other had accused in their bickering. Hot blood against his hand. He pulled the knife out. The second man yelped, stumbling back, pulling his own weapon.

Brenner yanked his knife from the bleeding gunman and flung it.

The blade buried into the throat of the second man. He stumbled, tripped over a root, and then—gurgling and bleeding—collapsed to the ground.

Both men hit the earth simultaneously, dying nearly instantly.

As Brenner left them bleeding in the mud, Abraham stared up at the ex-SEAL, wide-eyed and terrified. Brenner held a finger to his lips and began to turn sharply. But then he froze.

A *click*.

"Don't move a muscle!" snarled the one facing the lake.

Brenner's hands slowly raised. He swallowed hesitantly, wondering just how quickly he could draw his weapon. He felt confident, even with a gun on him already, he had a fifty-fifty shot of getting off a kill before he was downed.

But Ella had requested quiet.

If he started shooting, the whole mountain would know they were there.

She was underwater. Scything towards their victim. For what end? Who knew. But Ella had a way of arriving at a decision and willing it to work.

But now, as Brenner's back was to the gunman, he let out a shaking breath, his right leg twinging.

"Who are you?" the harsh voice snapped. "Speak—bastard, or I'll blow your head off! You know what. To hell with you—"

Brenner tensed, turning sharply, his own hand ripping his weapon from his holster. In the blink of an eye, lightning fast, the marshal had his gun raised, aimed and fi—

He held his fire, finger tense on the trigger, eyes wide.

Mortimer Graves was standing over a gurgling man, wiping a knife off on the fellow's suit, whistling softly as he did. For a moment, as Graves wiped his blade, it almost felt as if he'd forgotten anyone else was watching him.

Graves wore a pleased expression, his eyes hooded, his lips turned into something of a smirk. His whistling was quiet, gentle, like a lullaby. Graves knelt for a second by the side of the man he'd killed, stroking his hair the same way he had Abraham's.

"Psst," Brenner said, his eyes narrowed.

Graves looked up suddenly, freezing as if startled. He blinked a few times, like a predator who had found itself in a hunter's scope over a contested kill.

Brenner's own gun was still raised, pointed at Mortimer. He didn't lower it.

Graves stared at the weapon, at Brenner, then down at the dead man. "You're welcome," Mortimer said softly. He plucked the gunman's firearm off the ground, holding it tight in his unbloodied hand. "Shall we?" Graves asked, nodding around the edge of the lake towards where Rose was still struggling in the water, fending off one attacker and then the next. Some sort of ritual. The recruits were now trying to stab her to death.

Brenner exhaled in frustration. No time to dwell on Mortimer Graves, nor any desire to thank the weird creep. Though perhaps he deserved it.

The prickle down Brenner's back receded. And he shook his head, gesturing with his gun off to the side.

"Let's grab the storekeeper. Their leader."

"Chop off the head of the snake," Graves said quietly. "I like it."

The two men began to turn, Brenner shooting concerned looks towards the sacred body of water, searching desperately for a shadow, a ripple, for anything at—

"DAD!" Abraham screamed. "DAD, HELP!"

Brenner cursed, whirling about. Mortimer Graves didn't bother cursing, lunging forward and slamming his gun into the side of Abraham's temple. To the strange CI's credit, he didn't shoot or slash. But he did hit hard enough to knock the boy unconscious. Abraham collapsed to the ground now, motionless, laying on the earth amidst roots and pools of blood gathering on muddy terrain. The three corpses surrounding him were tell-tale of trouble when other scouts came to investigate.

"Abraham?" a voice yelled from across the shore. A desperate, thin and anxious voice. "Who's there?"

The store keeper snapped, "Jared? Damon?"

No response.

"I think we may have some unwanted guests..." the leader of the cult said, his voice resonant. "Hello? Whoever's out there—we come in peace... Let's speak, shall we? The moon is watching. The moon tells me... men? Two of you? Slinking in the woods. The moon tells me you're armed. You can't hide from the moon! You can't hide from *me*!"

Chanting now. A flurry of more footsteps. Shouting. The sound of running.

"That's not good," Brenner whispered.

Mortimer hissed sharply, looking one way, then the other. The two men instinctively began to retreat, moving back to the right, heading in the direction they'd come from.

But then more sounds. Thumping footsteps.

Brenner cursed, shooting a look back.

"Hey! Sorry we're late!" someone said. "Something happened in town!"

Figures... multiple—at least five—were emerging from the mountain pass. Effectively cutting off retreat. If they went left, around the lake, they'd cross an open field—easily being spotted. If they went right, they'd run into the cultists now racing towards them.

If they stayed put, they'd be found.

"Shit, shit," Brenner cursed. Where was Ella? Where was...

"What now?" Graves whispered.

Brenner glanced to the water, breathing heavily, and then made a rash decision. He reached out, snagging Graves' arm and tugging sharply.

Chapter 18

Ella's lungs protested the underwater swim. But she spotted moving shapes ahead of her. Legs in the water, stumbling back. A figure, a dark shadow, submerging more and more, chased further out into the sacred lake.

She swam more rapidly, hands extended, scooping the frigid cold and propelling her form through the murk. Ten feet in front of her, one of the figures, a man judging by the size of his legs and abdomen, was reaching towards Rose's retreating form. The young woman, in a panic, was now treading water, trying to swim. But she was out of breath—terrified.

Ella, in her mind, had thought it might work to pull Rose underwater and bring her back the way she'd come. But this was fanciful.

She hadn't approached with a plan, only with a certainty that she wasn't going to watch the young woman perish.

The water swirled and churned, bubbles fleeing as Ella kicked forward. Her hands shot out, snaring the thick calf of the red-robed figure pursuing Rose. She pulled sharply, and above she heard the sound of a muffled shout. The man splashed into the water, unbalanced. Ella's ribs grazed Rose's feet. Rose's head still barely above water. The young woman let out a terrified yelp at the sudden contact. Again, the sound was muffled by the water.

The four other cultist recruits hesitated now, no longer surging forward, but stumbling back. Confusion reigned briefly.

The man whom she'd tripped was fumbling, staring down at her now, his head still in the air, above the cold liquid. He gripped a knife in hand, which from her vantage point, floating five feet below the surface, looked little more than a streak of silver.

This glimmering blade slashed into the water, like a trout darting beneath the surface.

She yelled and kicked out, bubbles fleeing from her unbidden shout as she tried to fling herself sideways. But there was nothing for traction—save Rose.

Ella kicked off the younger woman, but the knife still grazed her ribs, coming close and slicing down along Ella's flank. She hissed in pain but managed to exchange a killing blow for a scrape. At the same time, still thrashing in the lake, her hands shot out, grabbing the attacker by the knife-wielding wrist.

Every motion seemed slower now. Every kick and movement and lurch in the water impeded somewhat by the viscosity. Still, she wrangled for the knife.

Her lungs were fit to burst.

She'd lost her air.

Had thrown herself into a wolf den with no way out. But Ella's adrenaline was still racing. Her heart still pounding. She managed to press on the pressure points in the large man's wrist, causing him to yelp and drop his knife. She pulled it free.

And then surged up, her head emerging from the lake. Her feet barely found the silty floor. Small, petite, *short*—just some of the terms that had been applied to her over the years.

And now, she was struggling—this deep—to keep her head above water.

Rose was behind Ella now, whimpering and gasping and spitting cold liquid. Ella shot a quick glance back, trying to make it a comforting one.

But now, a voice from the platform was shouting out—Dawkins' voice, "Don't let the foreigner spill blood in the sacred lake!" he screamed. "The sacrifice is yours! Take it!"

The five cultists neck-deep in the water, occasionally hopping and elevating themselves by spreading their arms and treading, all glared at Ella. Abraham's father stood the furthest back and kept scanning the trees, a look of concern and fear in his eyes.

The deputy she recognized, though, was just scowling at her, his knife gripped tight. The blood from where they'd cut their arms swirled in the liquid about them, staining the lake in streaks of crimson. Ribbons of red fluttered out, like the tendrils of some inky squid attempting to wrap around Ella and Rose.

"Stay close," Ella whispered.

The other red-cloaked figures on the shore were boasting weapons. Many of them pointing their guns at the water. But none of them fired yet. They looked hesitantly on at the strange scene, but would then shoot glances towards Dawkins, searching for input.

The one thing about those who followed a charismatic leader—in her experience, their minds were malleable. They *needed* permission to act.

Perhaps they didn't want to shoot into their sacred lake.

Briefly, Ella considered putting the knife to Rose's neck as a bluff. They didn't want a stranger to bleed the woman in the lake, so perhaps that meant if Ella pretended to threaten her, they'd hold their fire.

But she abandoned this consideration. For one, Rose was terrified. There was no telling what the woman would do if threatened again. But also, Ella wasn't sure this ploy would work.

But taking a hostage in general? It seemed the only course.

She had the big man's knife.

And so she went in, fast.

She didn't give anyone time to think—least of all herself. Water speck-led her face, pouring down her blonde hair, which plastered to her forehead.

She lashed out with her knife, cutting sharply towards the large man she'd disarmed.

He yelped, trying to retreat, but she managed to catch him by his stupid, oversized, billowing cloak. If moving underwater for her had been cumbersome, for this large galoot in his ballooning bathrobe, it was even more of an impediment.

She snatched at his collar, dragging him forward.

Except... he was twice her size. So what happened was, she dragged herself forward. He tried to grab at her wrist with the knife, but she slashed his palm, drawing more blood.

No polite smiles. No deference and concealed emotions. Now, all she wanted was to *act*.

And so she put her knife against the man's neck, pressing it hard. "Don't move!" she snarled. Louder, she repeated the instruction. "Don't move!"

The *or else* was implied by the blade jammed into their comrade's neck.

But she wasn't done either. A single pressure point? Perhaps avoid-able? But multiple? The big man in front of her, who she vaguely recognized from the lake in Parcel, had frozen stiff, his hands outstretched, palm and forearm bleeding. Small droplets pattered the surface of the water around him, tap-tap-tapping.

The second pressure point came in the form of a comment. "Abraham is in the trees," she said, her voice harsh, low. "Six men with guns have their weapons pressed to his head as we speak," she added, her voice still shaking in anger. "If you don't drop that knife *now,* they have orders to kill him."

Abraham's father went stock still, staring at her.

The others, close enough to hear what she'd said, also froze.

Rose was gasping behind Ella and had retreated a few more steps. Now she was kicking and treading water to keep her head out of the liquid. But at this comment, she drifted closer again. Not only, Ella suspected, out of a sense of security for the angry lady with the knife threatening her aggressors but also because the ground was higher and she could stand to breathe.

At the mention of Abraham, though, Rose stammered a question. "Is—is he okay?"

Ella just gave a quick shake of her head but kept her knife wedged under the man's neck while her eyes pierced Abraham's father where he stood.

The silence reigned over the scene, and everyone shifted nervously.

Dawkins, at the mention of gunmen, had begun to retreat along the wooden bridge, hastening towards the *Forbidden* sign, stepping over a chain and joining his lackeys amidst the trees. At least ten handguns with a couple of rifles and sawed-offs were pointed at the water, at Ella.

It was a powder keg. A hair trigger could detonate this whole thing into one horrific massacre.

But Ella didn't blink, didn't back down. Instead, facing the guns, past the big man's face, she shouted out, "Put your weapons down! We have you surrounded."

She shivered now, tense. Off to her left, she thought she spotted movement, but there was simply too much to keep track of. Her knife had kept the big man in place. Her words had stopped Abraham's father. But the three *other* Parcel recruits? The ones who'd also bled their arms?

They had finally regrouped. Their eyes narrowed. One of them whispered something to another. And slowly, they began to move towards her.

Three knives against one. And the big man would join in too if she left him.

Shit... shit... Ella tried to think what to do.

She shouted, "FBI!" Flashing her badge with her other hand.

But this didn't work either. Like hounds at the scent of meat, an owner's command did little to penetrate the fog of desire.

And they wanted their meat bloody.

***

Brenner Gunn didn't move, frozen in place and wincing. He strained in exertion, sweat pouring down his face, his arms shaking horribly from the exertion of remaining aloft. His hands were on fire—scraped and cut from his hasty climb.

They hadn't been able to go left or right, across the open field. The lake wasn't an option either, at least not at first, not when Ella had asked for silence.

So they'd done the only thing they could.

Climb.

Mortimer Graves had gone first. The man had proved able and nimble enough and now crouched in a lower y-branch above. A few flecks of bark had skittered down Brenner's shirt collar, itching at his back like prickles from a fresh haircut. His own climb had been far faster. He simply hadn't had time to take it slow.

And the reason was evident below them.

Five figures clutching heavy firearms. Two M-16s set to burst fire by the look of them. A scoped rifle. And two AR-15s. The big firepower had finally arrived.

These figures were wearing the same red as the cultists but in the form of hooded sweatshirts and slacks rather than robes, allowing for mobility. They also had radios on their shoulders and one, the leader—a tall man with brown hair, who looked suspiciously like the cult leader—had a device in his ear.

Brothers? Cousins? The familial relationship seemed apparent.

And something else was also apparent.

The cult had private security patrolling the mountains. And now, these five heavily armed figures—who likely had little else to do in the mountains besides practice their aim—had come to a stop directly *beneath* where Brenner and Graves were hiding.

Brenner's arms were braced on a branch, holding tight. He hadn't managed to completely climb up before they'd arrived, and when he'd heard the crunch of branch and twig beneath him, he'd frozen stiff, not wanting to attract any attention.

And now, feeling much like one of those silly cat posters with titles like *Hang in There,* he held on for dear life, his muscles straining, trembling. He could feel blood rushing to his face from the exertion of staying aloft, half on the branch, but his legs and lower part of his abdomen still dangling fifteen feet off the ground.

The branch was starting to *creak* from the renewed strain. He cursed silently, readjusted his grip and small bits of bark scattered, leaves tumbling as well, fluttering to the ground.

For the moment, no one seemed to notice. But Brenner's breath came in wild and rapid gasps. He pressed his teeth tightly together, his gun was back in his holster. Ella's gun tucked into his belt.

Mortimer had occupied a far more secure position above him and was extending a hand to help Brenner rise.

But Brenner shook his head. Not simply because of how distasteful it might be to touch that man's hand but because any further movement, sound or motion could alert the figures below to the presence of the intruders above them.

The five heavily armed men, though, were momentarily distracted by the unconscious form of Abraham.

"Hey," said the leader, who looked like a family member of Dawkins. His combat boot prodded at Abraham's fallen form. "Hey, you!" he said, louder, still poking with the toe of his muddy boot.

The four others gathered around, glancing at the ground, and then exclaiming as they spotted the corpses.

"Soney—come in, Soney!" said the leader, pressing a finger to his ear to secure his radio receiver. "Hey, do you copy?" A pause. More leaves and strands of bark fluttered down. One leaf even grazed the leader's head and landed on the scope of his rifle where it rested in the crook of his arm. "Yeah—not good. We got bodies here. Brothers—three of them. And then Helen's kid. Yeah. He's alive."

Suddenly, there was the sound of shouting. Splashing. A disturbance in the lake behind them, but Brenner couldn't turn to look.

The tall leader went still, still listening to some unheard voice. "What do you mean?" he demanded, scowling.

But Brenner wasn't privy to the radio receiver's response. Now, the five figures were staring out towards the lake, raising their weapons and approaching the shoreline. Brenner's eyes bulged. He kicked a bit more, his muscles—involuntarily—twinging and trembling violently.

The figures below stepped over the corpses of their comrades, occasionally shooting glances down. As they passed, each man touched fingers to their foreheads then pointed the digit at the dead before murmuring some prayer beneath their breath.

Brenner was losing his grip now.

The gunmen were directly below. The tall man with the radio receiver was hastening away from Abraham's unconscious form to join his men on the shoreline now. Each of them raised their weapons in turn.

And as they did, Brenner spotted their target.

As he continued to slip, his scraped hands struggling to keep a grip on the loose branch, his legs kicking above the threat, he glimpsed through the lower branches what was transpiring in the lake, about three hundred yards away.

Ella had emerged from the water—distinguishable at this distance by her blond hair. Plus, she was the only one walking *towards* the threat. The others recoiled, reeling back.

He watched as Ella grappled with a large man, pressed a knife to his neck and then shouted something to the others. He watched the flash of the badge in her hand, raised above her head.

He watched as the cult leader beat a hasty retreat across the dock, back towards his underlings on the shore.

Now, the gunmen below were stabilizing themselves against trees, branches, aiming towards where Ella and Rose Lewis were nearly submerged, only their heads emerging from the lake. But Ella didn't notice the gunmen behind her. Couldn't notice.

She was too distracted by four times as many gunmen on shore, by the knife-wielding recruits trudging towards her once more, slowly, cautiously, but determinedly.

The five high-powered cultists behind her didn't catch her eye. Or if they did, she couldn't focus on them.

And so Brenner had to make a choice. They were all far better armed than he was. But on the other hand...

They didn't know he was there.

Besides, his damn arms were going to sleep, and if he didn't do something soon, he'd lose all the skin on his fingers where they scraped against the rough branch.

And so, he dropped.

Fifteen feet. Allowing his legs to buckle to avoid cracking anything. He was already shooting *before* he landed. Having pulled his weapon from his holster *mid-fall* and then aiming and firing just as his feet hit the dirt.

Fall. Aim, shoot. Hit the ground, knees buckle. Shoot. Shoot. Pain in his right leg. Ignored. Shoot.

Four men dropped dead in a matter of two seconds. The final one, the leader of the group with the radio receiver spun around, eyes wide, weapon rising. The sound of the gunshots only *just* registering as Brenner straightened up.

He glared as leaves tumbled and branches fell. He pointed his gun at the man with the scoped rifle. "Dawson is your brother?" he asked simply.

The man with the rifle had frozen, his gun still facing the ground.

"Is he your *brother*?" Brenner snapped. "Radio him. Tell him to back off the lake or—"

But the red-garbed fighter wasn't in the negotiating mood. He cursed, snarled and raised his weapon. Brenner put two in his chest before the gunman had a chance to squeeze off a shot.

But now they were in it. Gunfire was the single best way to arouse the ire of a shore full of cultists.

And so Brenner sprinted forward, hopping over two of the men he'd just killed, snatching the scoped rifle from where it had fallen on the leading guard's chest, and—after finagling the shoulder strap—he raised it, aimed and then cursed.

Ella was surging back, diving under the water. Gunfire had erupted from the shore. A bullet caught Rose and she stumbled with a faint shout. All mayhem broke loose in the lake.

"God dammit!" Brenner raised his weapon and gestured at Graves. "Hey—hey get down from there. I need that. No, dammit-*that*!" he pointed sharply, his weapon now wedged against a nub five feet up the tree. "Give it to me now!"

Chapter 19

The gunfire erupted behind Ella like a storm of thunder.

The reactions on the shore were nearly instantaneous. Perhaps they thought her badge raised above her head was a gun. Perhaps they were simply startled by the sudden noise.

Whatever the case, the return fire from the Spring Children peppered the lake. Two of the new recruits were shot in the back. The deputy's shout of pain was cut short as he stumbled into the water, face down. He didn't rise.

The other Parcel recruits flung themselves sideways. Ella still didn't know this strange, symbiotic relationship between the townies of Parcel and the cultists in the mountains, but as far as she could tell, some deal—an arrangement—had been struck between the two groups for years. *You give me female virgins to sacrifice, and I give you a place in the Spring Children.*

Whatever parasitic arrangement had been struck, it was secondary to the oath of gunfire.

The large man whom she'd pressed the knife to was also shot.

But the bullets were meant for her. For Rose.

Ella was small—and this saved her. The big man she was using as something of a meat shield caught more lead. Other bullets zipped into the water around her, causing small splashes or miniature geysers of liquid.

Rose yelled in pain as a bullet cut through her shoulder. She hit the water, and Ella cursed, leaping back, grabbing the young woman by the leg and pulling her towards the dead recruit.

She then submerged.

It wasn't a pleasant experience to use a dead cultist recruit as a barricade. But the only cover she had came in the form of the gun-shot corpse.

And so she dove under it, taking Rose—who was protesting weakly—with her.

The two women camped under the floating body. More bullets zipped around them, scything through the liquid like darting minnows. More bullets hit the body above her.

But the small caliber weaponry from the shore didn't manage to penetrate the corpse.

Ella struggled to see as she tread water, inches below the floating dead man. Rose was bleeding, the red trails extending around her, flitting on the liquid, clouding the water even further.

Ella hissed. She needed to get Rose to the shore. Needed to stop the bleeding.

But the gunfire rained down on them. Ella had left her own weapon with Brenner. Was that who'd caused those gunshots earlier?

She remained motionless under the water, trembling, eyes prickling.

And then the gunfire ceased.

Ella listened, her ears full of water, her head constantly bumping against the floating corpse above her. But no more bullets.

A sudden, strange silence.

Ella's heart pounded, her lungs followed a similar rhythm, fit to burst. She wanted to emerge, but what if it was a ploy?

What if, at any moment, a bullet might lodge into her?

Her hand gripped Rose's wrist, holding on tight. Her lungs were already protesting, as she hadn't had time to inhale deeply in her rush to take cover.

But even as these thoughts spiked through her, Ella realized she couldn't stay there forever. Slowly, she pushed her head around the side of the body.

She waited, listening. And then emerged, breathing shakily, still wedged against the corpse in case she needed to submerge again.

All quiet.

She then looked up, over. Two figures were splashing towards her. Unarmed, their hands raised. Their faces were hidden behind their masks. She snarled and raised her knife, pointing at them threateningly.

But they kept coming and didn't falter.

As they drew nearer, they were saying, "We'll help! Don't attack—we're helping!"

Ella blinked, water pouring down her face, droplets falling from her eyelashes. The knife trembled where she gripped it. Her other hand still held onto Rose. But the young woman was still submerged. Unconscious? Worse?

Ella felt a snarl forming on her lips. She slashed the knife a couple of times. But the two figures held out their hands as if in surrender. They paused, dripping, ten feet away, glancing back to the shore.

But then Dawson's voice called out. "Bring her to the shore! Bind her wound!"

Ella stared at the leader of the cult. The two cultists continued forward, ignoring Ella and her knife, as if it couldn't touch them. Or, as if they simply had no choice.

They tried to grab at Rose, but Ella slashed one on the knuckles. The cultist cursed, whipping her hand back. But she reached out again.

"She'll die if you don't let us!" Dawson called on the shore.

Ella was still confused. But she watched closely as the two figures in the water gently lifted Rose from the lake. They pulled her towards the shore, tugging insistently as Ella still held on to the young woman.

And then she spotted the leader.

Dawson, who she was confident had once upon a time gone by the name Dawkins, was standing on the wooden dock again, hands raised. Not in some prayer or a priestly exultation, but in surrender.

And fear.

Though he was still directing the figures in the water, he was frozen stiff as cordwood. Ella breathed slowly, droplets flecking the rippling and agitated surface of the lake. Last she'd seen, the cult leader had been fleeing to the woods. Her eyes traced to the tree where he'd been sheltering.

It was gone.

At least, two of the thick, arm-sized branches were gone, dangling by splinters. And now she realized Dawson was clutching at his shoulder, blood streaming through his fingers, staining the back of his hand and running like a current down his forearm, towards his wrist and along his fingers.

He'd been shot.

By one of his own?

No... no, he was murmuring as if praying. Not praying, she realized. Talking on a radio. The small mic was attached to his lapel, and he angled his face down, speaking into it.

Over the sound of gasping and the thrashing of the two reluctant helpers, Ella heard. "Alright—I've done as you asked. Now what?"

Ella turned slowly, being dragged along now while she still gripped Rose's leg. But she spotted a glint of metal. A man on the opposite shore, a scoped rifle aimed *directly* at Dawkins. She heard the faintest sound of static.

Somehow, Brenner was communicating with a radio in the cult leader's ear.

He had his rifle trained directly on the man in red. By the looks of things, he'd shot Dawkins' cover, then shot his arm, and then threatened him until he stepped forward again, out into the open.

The threat was clear.

Do anything to hurt Ella or Rose, and I'll blow your brains out.

Ella felt a slow flicker of release, and she let out a long sigh of relief. Hesitantly, eyes still on Dawkins, studying the fear in his eyes, she swam around the floating corpse of the gun-riddled recruit. She swam after Rose and her two "rescuers," kicking slowly. The cultists dragged Rose onto the shore and hastily began bandaging her shoulder. Rose was breathing, slowly, water spilling down her features, her eyes fluttering and her voice coming in slow, stuttered murmurs.

She faced the dark night sky, laying in the mud, amidst the tangle of large roots. The two cultists who'd been sent by their leader moved with deft hands, suggesting some level of experience with binding wounds. Vets? Doctors?

Ella still didn't quite understand this strange place.

Now, she was standing on the silty, soft ground, wading through the water, carefully approaching the shore. All eyes were on her.

Brenner was still covering her, his scoped rifle aimed at the head of the snake.

Without its head, the body didn't move.

Twenty or more red-cloaked figures stood on the shore, guns lowered at the ground, motionless, watching Ella, watching their leader, and occasionally, pointing across the lake towards where the sniper was keeping an eye on all of them.

Rose was murmuring something now. Her shoulder bandaged, the young woman was soaked to the bone, shivering and crying at the same time.

"Abraham," whispered a voice on the shore. "Where's my son?"

Ella shot a look at Abraham's father—she still didn't know his name. But she knew that he was responsible for depositing the clothing and luggage of victims in the well on his property. That's what Abraham had said. Helen, the matriarch, was the one who'd cut her own son's ear for "betraying" the town. The "elders."

Ella shot a look towards Dawkins. The would-be shopkeeper at the general store. At least *one* of the elders, she guessed, was now standing frozen, bleeding and trembling in the sights of an ex-Navy SEAL.

A lull had fallen across the makeshift battlefield. Rose was being tended to. And in that brief moment, Ella felt a slow, growing confidence. They'd make it out alive.

She stared at the man on the dock, frowning, dripping. She shot a quick glance at Rose, making sure the young woman was safe.

She said, "Who in town knows about this?"

Dawkins looked at her. His eyes held that same, cold quality that lived in Mortimer's. He shook his head. "No one."

"You're lying."

He nodded. "Do you know the summer's song, child?"

"Is the sheriff involved? People in town *must* know about this—about *you*."

"Do you know the heartbeat of winter?"

She took another step onto the shore, stopping long enough to pick up a fallen handgun, which one of the medics seemed to have dropped.

She hefted it. A few of the other cultists on the shore watched uneasily.

It was all going to plan. Dawkins said, "For years we've had an understanding with Parcel. Many of my children live in those homes. On those shores. You... *FBI* have no authority here," he spat in contempt but then winced, still gripping his shoulder.

Ella had supposed as much. What a mess.

Some of the Spring Children lived uncloaked among the town... The deputy was a recruit. So the sheriff? No... No, he'd been scared of the name *Dawkins*. Unless, of course, he was their lackey, going along with it.

Helen though? Perhaps.

Whatever the case, she needed to reach the helicopter. Call in on the SAT—this time with probable cause. And then rush Rose to a hospital.

It all weighed on her, but she took another trudging step from the water, which sucked and swirled as she stepped onto the shore, gun in hand.

And that's when everything went to hell.

***

Brenner aimed his sniper across the water, fixated on the leader of the cult, speaking into the radio receiver he'd taken off Dawson's brother's body.

"Not an inch, remember," Brenner muttered quietly. "Stand on your mark—move at all, and I'll hit you again."

He kept his eyes fixated on the figures across the water.

And that's when he felt the faintest of breaths against his cheek. A soft voice, "I said I wouldn't hurt a hair on his head."

Brenner hesitated, frowning but keeping his gaze attentively on the threat across the lake. "What?" Brenner muttered.

"Not a hair on his head," Mortimer said again. "So I'd best aim for the chest then, hmm?"

"What?" Brenner shot a quick look back.

Mortimer was holding one of the M-16s. Gripping it tight and standing on the shore, the weapon raised, pointing across the water.

Brenner frowned. "Hey—hey, hang on. What are you doing?"

Mortimer spoke quietly, his voice resonate. "I made a promise once. A different promise. Long ago. I intend to keep it."

"Hey... hey—HEY!"

Graves fired twice. Both shots hit the cult leader in the chest. The man stumbled—Brenner heard his pained gasp over the radio. And then Dawson fell forward, splashing into the lake. The same lake where he'd intended to murder Rose Lewis, the same lake now serving as the tomb of other victims floating face down.

Brenner was moving fast, gun whirling around. But he'd been taken off guard. Too focused on keeping Ella safe.

The butt of Graves' gun would have slammed into Brenner's skull if he hadn't moved faster than the blow. He slipped, though. His own gun raising. Mortimer dove back.

Brenner fired—hit a tree exactly where Graves' heart would've been. He sighed again—he wouldn't miss a second time.

"I'll shoot him," Graves said simply.

Brenner went still, gasping. Graves' gun was pointed at Abraham's unconscious forehead. The suit-wearing maniac watched Brenner with those cold eyes. "Lower it."

Brenner cursed.

Graves nodded and then turned, sprinting through the woods, placing another large tree between them.

Brenner aimed but was distracted now. Gunshots behind him.

"Shit!" he spun around, heart pounding, sniper raised, aiming across the lake where Ella was under fire.

Chapter 20

One moment, everything had been going well. Dawkins—the head of the snake—had been frozen on the bridge, reciting whatever commands he'd been given to the rest of his flock.

The next, his chest exploded and he splashed into the lake.

All hell broke loose.

Half the cultists ran. Wailing, moaning and screaming. The sight of their leader so easily felled clearly taking the wind from their sails.

The others let loose on Rose and Ella.

Ella moved fast. She shot a man aiming a shotgun at Rose's fallen form then surged forward, shoving into one of the medics, who—at the sudden commotion—reached down as if to strangle Rose.

Ella's shoulder caught the woman's chest, sending her reeling. A bullet meant for Ella caught the medic instead, dropping her.

The second would-be caretaker leapt into the lake, screaming as he swam towards his fallen leader. Others abandoned their guns and dove in to save their bleeding shepherd.

But at least seven still remained on shore, guns pointing and riddling the mud and lake with bullets.

Ella hit another.

Two more fell—shots from across the lake.

This gave her just enough time, gasping, to drag Rose's newly bandaged form around the side of the nearest tree, pulling her desperately under cover. Both the women were slim, small. The thick, jutting tree roots they'd spotted earlier served as earthworks, protecting them from gunfire.

Ella shot back. Shouting—grunts of pain. Wailing as others ran off into the mountains. Still others splashing, flailing desperately to *save* their already dead leader.

Brenner kept the suppressing fire.

Another figure emerged from behind a tree, pistol aimed at where Ella had taken cover. He fired. Wood chips and mud spattered her cheeks where the bullet struck the root.

But he then jolted back, a red hole having appeared directly between his eyes.

Ella kept low now, allowing Brenner—who was certainly the best shot she knew—to pick off the untrained, panicked Spring Children.

More shouting. More thumping footsteps.

Rose's desperate voice pleading, "P-please... I don't want to die. Where's Abe?"

"Shh," Ella whispered. "Keep quiet. You're going to be fine. I promise. You're going to be—"

Another loud blast. And then more silence.

Ella listened, quiet, waiting. No more noise. Leaves falling about her, twigs blasted by bullets and tumbling. The weeping figures on the shore had pulled Dawson onto the muddy terrain and were trying to bind him.

But he didn't move. Ella stared at where they were attempting to revive their leader. Her eyes fixated. No more gunshots. Brenner was either out of ammo or had determined there were no further threats.

Ella held Rose up, slowly, propping her against the tree.

She stared at the young woman then gestured around the lake, away from where the remaining Spring Children had gathered. "Run," Ella said. "Get to the other side of the lake. I'll cover for you." Ella stared at where the cult leader lay. Was he breathing?

She pressed a hand to her handcuffs. Nothing irked her more than allowing a bad guy to get away.

She'd done it before.

But not again.

Back on the mountains, in the snow, she'd wanted to find the killer...
Not her cousin who was out in a blizzard. But Ella had wanted to catch
the bad guy rather than save the victim.

It went deep. Apprehending monsters in the dark. She couldn't let
them get away. She refused. Already, figures were fleeing now, scattered, sprinting off into the mountains, to whatever hiding holes they
had.

The further she let them go, the worse.

Now, she cursed, watching as the three unarmed cultists who'd dove
to save their leader, lifted him on their shoulders and began struggling
up the bank, hastening away from the sacred lake.

They were getting away. She had to follow. She had—

"No. Please," Rose whispered.

Ella looked over.

The young woman's eyes were filled with panic. She lay on the roots,
one arm braced against the nearest lump as if it were some sort of
armrest. The makeshift bandage applied to her shoulder, wrapped
tight but already stained red.

Ella exhaled slowly, shooting a glance off after the retreating figures.
The leader of the cult, carried away. No more gunshots from Brenner.
He was letting them leave.

She couldn't. Could she?

"Please," Rose whispered again.

Ella's hand gripped her gun. Her knuckles rubbed against the cuffs on her belt. She thought of Maddie Porter. Of her sister, storming off into the blizzard.

Ella growled slowly, shaking her head, then turning. She slipped her arm under Rose's. "Alright. Let's go," she murmured.

She propped Rose up, helping the young woman to her feet. And then, carefully, avoiding the rough, slick terrain, she turned her back on the fleeing killers. Turned her back on the hunt.

And instead, slowly—so painstakingly slowly—she led Rose around the lake, retreating towards where she had left Graves and Brenner.

***

Ella watched as blue shirts with bright, yellow FBI logos excited the three helicopters. The wind disheveled her hair. And she leaned against the wooden porch of the general store.

Brenner was behind the counter—the same counter where they'd first encountered Dawson. The ex-soldier was helping himself to more meat sticks.

The two of them watched silently as a stretcher hastily carried Rose Lewis' form towards one of the emergency birds.

Ella kept the door propped open behind her. It had taken them an hour to reach the general store. The helicopters had appeared out of nowhere... Someone had already called them.

Who?

As they'd arrived, sheltering in the store, she'd heard the whir of blades against the night. Had glimpsed spotlights flying overhead. The people of Parcel hadn't come to investigate, preferring to stay in their lumber homes, hidden from sight.

Out of sight, out of mind.

They'd lived decades with such an adage.

The grove filled with bodies attested to this. Sometimes, all someone had to do to know the truth was to look up.

But it was far more comfortable to stare at the ground.

"So tell me again," Ella said slowly, wincing as she moved her neck, still soaked. The trek on the ATV through the mountains had dried her somewhat, but now she was trembling horribly. "He just shot the guy and left?"

"Said something about a hair on the head," Brenner muttered. "I didn't get it."

Ella hesitated, glancing back. "He didn't harm a hair on Dawkins' head."

"What?"

"Nothing."

"Who the hell is that guy, Ella?"

"Well, well, well," a voice said as two figures approached where they sheltered in the General Store.

Ella glanced over and then frowned.

She watched as a mirror image of herself marched over. The woman wore seashell earrings—bright silver this time with diamonds. She also wore an expensive jacket and designer slacks. The man at her side—a tall fellow with a politician's face—had a police uniform on.

"Cilla," Ella said, nodding slowly. "Baker," she said, glancing at the chief of police from Nome.

At least ten FBI agents were now hastening towards Parcel, moving quickly. A woman in an FBI jacket was approaching, frowning as she did.

Ella winced. She recognized the woman. A supervising agent from Seattle. A no-nonsense, tough-as-nails sort. The sort that would cause more career trouble if Ella wasn't careful.

The woman was hesitating though, pausing to speak with a few agents, directing them as she consulted something on her phone.

And so Ella slunk back, disappearing into the shadows of the shop.

Which of course meant Priscilla followed. Always one to shine a light on anything someone else wanted concealed.

Priscilla crossed her arms, her eyes defiant—when were they not—her chin pushed out. "An hour ago we get a distress signal from up here—with *your* badge number," Cilla said, frowning at Ella. "Figures. So what's this about armed militia?"

Ella hesitated, glancing at Brenner, who shrugged.

"Graves," Ella murmured.

The serial killer had murdered another. Had fled. But had managed to call in backup. Perhaps that was what he'd been doing when he'd slipped Brenner. Before they'd even *known* about the armed killers. Before they'd known about an inevitable gunfight, Graves had the wherewithal to make a call.

And to use Ella's badge to do it.

"Why did so many show up?" Ella asked quietly. "So quickly?" She trailed off.

Cilla nodded. "Good question," the woman said with a snort. "And no—before it goes to your head—it wasn't for you. The Mayor called it in."

"What?"

"The mayor in Nome called it in. A favor. Told us to move fast—called his friend the governor in Seattle."

"The mayor..." Ella trailed off. She blinked in confusion. A slow dread crept up her spine. A favor... for a campaign donor, maybe? A very wealthy, very connected donor? Her mind flitted to the Graveyard Killer, and another surge of fear accompanied it. *Who* was this man?

Priscilla shrugged. "Some campaign donor asked him to. Friends in high places, Ella. Someone's finally learning how to play the game."

She patted her sister on the cheek, then snatched a stick of biltong. The same spicy Peri Peri flavor Brenner had grabbed.

Priscilla peeled back the wrapper, and Brenner—who hadn't been looking—lowered his own in disgust, tossing it into the bin behind the counter.

Baker was watching it all with a frown, shaking his head. "We need to debrief you both," Baker said. "Special Agent Crawford is on point."

He gestured and Ella sighed. It would take time—likely weeks—to round up the cultists in the mountains. Even longer to find out who in Parcel was involved, who *knew*. She wondered if Rose Lewis would tattle on Abraham for his involvement. They would need a witness to Abe's participation.

To all of it.

Ella nodded and exhaled slowly.

She felt a weight of guilt and then stepped from inside the shop.

Brenner followed.

"Hey there, big guy," Cilla said cheerfully.

"Bite me," Brenner retorted, brushing past.

"That an offer?" Cilla said, chewing on her biltong.

Brenner ignored her, and together, Ella and Brenner stepped off the porch, approaching the SA in order to start the long process of unwinding miles of red tape.

"Brenner," Ella whispered as she approached.

"Hmm?"

"Don't mention Graves."

"How's that?"

"Just someone we met. Gave us a ride. Kay?"

He shot her a look, frowning.

She looked back at him, allowing the worry she was *feeling* to cross her countenance. It felt more costly to show the emotion than to simply communicate it.

But as Brenner watched her, he then shrugged. "Fine. Deal."

The two of them stood side by side, pausing halfway to the makeshift helipads as the supervising agent marched towards them.

Epilogue:

Soney Dawkins was dead.

Ella frowned through the window of the helicopter, peering down at the mountains as they lifted up, up, over. Morning sunlight was now spreading across the horizon.

Brenner leaned against the opposite window, sleeping quietly, his blonde-brown hair winking like spun gold where it pressed to the chilly window.

Below, Ella thought she spotted more blue jackets moving through the trees. Towards the sacred lake. Eight bodies had been recovered. Fifteen cultists, arrested. Two townspeople. Including Larry—the young man Brenner had punched.

But the red tape was still unwinding.

They hadn't mentioned Graves. Had been vague about the "tip" that had led them here. But Ella could feel the breath against the nape of her neck.

The more eyeballs on her, the worse it would get.

And if anyone higher-up found out about the Graveyard Killer?

She shivered in horror, staring down and wondering if someone in the village would be able to provide a good enough description of Mortimer. If they did... it would lead right back to her.

No one knew what the Graveyard Killer looked like, though. She was the one who'd caught him. She'd never revealed his identity.

She shook her head, sighing and leaning back in the seat.

Rose Lewis had been busy at the nearest hospital, in Nome, healing and pointing out her attackers. Already, her testimony had led to five more arrests.

But she hadn't said anything about Abraham's involvement.

And so neither had Ella.

She wasn't sure if she would... but Abe had paid a price to bring them to rescue Rose. It was all too much, and she was far too tired to decide what to do until she made an official statement.

Besides...

Other things were on Ella's mind.

She shifted uncomfortably in the helicopter seat, breathing softly.

Her mind was on the phone.

The Graveyard Killer had proven he couldn't be trusted. She should've known. He'd come to this town with one goal—to kill. And she'd helped him.

But he'd saved her life, and at the time, he'd given her the phone of the assassin.

The man he'd eventually disposed of.

Someone had taken a shot at her in her motel room. Had waited for her to return.

Someone had hired this person. And she was determined to find out *who*. The phone was still back at her motel... But first thing on landing, before giving her full report, she would ship the phone.

Ship it back to Quantico.

If anyone could open the thing, it was Guyves—her old partner there. A friend, after a fashion. Either way, Ella was determined to find out who'd hired the assassin.

And as for Graves?

She raised her own phone, intent on deleting his number and blocking it for good. But only then did she realize... the thing was soaked. Dead as a doorknob.

Her night-time swim had drowned it.

She stared out the window again, watching as more blue coats moved up the mountains in groups of five, guns raised.

Within a few days, a week… maybe more… the rest of the Spring Children would be captured. The participants in Parcel would be found.

Ella could only hope that the pointing fingers didn't eventually lead back to her.

A crackle of static. The pilot glanced back. "Hey—boss wants to talk to you."

She stared. "Umm… the SA?"

The pilot nodded.

"About what?"

The pilot held up a finger, pressed the headset a bit, adjusting it, then turned back. "Do you know someone named Mortimer Graves?"

Ella's heart skipped a beat. She went quiet, staring.

She opened her mouth; closed it again.

She just stared, frozen, uncertain what to say. How to react.

"Do you?" the pilot insisted. "SA wants to know. Actually—shit, hang on. She says she found someone down there. Gonna have to speak with you back at base."

Ella let out a faint, little sigh, nodding and closing her eyes instantly as if to block out the world.

Inwardly, though, her heart was pattering. Her pulse, racing.

Do you know someone named Mortimer Graves?

It was all crashing down. The house of cards was tumbling.

And she was going to be debriefed in Nome.

She supposed it made sense that her life would eventually fall apart back in her hometown. Destiny some might call it.

A cruel twist of fate others might say.

One thing was certain—her family would be more than happy to wave goodbye if Ella was hauled off in cuffs.

Other Books by Georgia Wagner

The skeletons in her closet are twitching... Genius chessmaster and FBI consultant Artemis Blythe swore she'd never return to the misty Cascade Mountains. Her father—a notorious serial killer, responsible for the deaths of seven women—is now imprisoned, in no small part due to a clue she provided nearly fifteen years ago. And now her father wants his vengeance. A new serial killer is hunting the wealthy and the elite in the town of Pinelake. Artemis' father claims he knows the identity of the killer, but he'll only tell daughter dearest. Against her will, she finds herself forced back to her old stomping grounds.Once known as a child chess prodigy, now the locals only think of her as 'The Ghostkiller's' daughter.In the face of a shamed family name and a brother involved with the Seattle mob, Artemis endeavors to use her tactical genius to solve the baffling case.Hunting a murderer who strikes without a trace, if she fails, the next skeleton in her closet will be her own.

Want to know more?

Greenfield press is the brainchild of bestselling author Steve Higgs. He specializes in writing fast paced adventurous mystery and urban fantasy with a humorous lilt. Having made his money publishing his own work, Steve went looking for a few 'special' authors whose work he believed in.

Georgia Wagner was the first of those, but to find out more and to be the first to hear about new releases and what is coming next, you can join the Facebook group by copying the following link into your browser - www.facebook.com/GreenfieldPress.

About the Author

Georgia Wagner worked as a ghost writer for many, many years before finally taking the plunge into self-publishing. Location and character are two big factors for Georgia, and getting those right allows the story to flow seamlessly onto the page. And flow it does, because Georgia is so prolific a new term is required to describe the rate at which nerve-tingling stories find their way into print.

When not found attached to a laptop, Georgia likes spending time in local arboretums, among the trees and ponds. An avid cultivator of orchids, begonias, and all things floral, Georgia also has a strong penchant for art, paintings, and sculptures. A many-decades long passion for mystery novels and years of chess tournament experience makes Georgia the perfect person to pen the Artemis Blythe series.

More Books By Steve Higgs

Printed in Great Britain
by Amazon